TRAIL MAGIC

A LESBIAN ROMANCE

CARA MALONE

Copyright © 2018 by Cara Malone

All rights reserved.

No part of this book may be reproduced in any form or by any electronic or mechanical means, including information storage and retrieval systems, without written permission from the author, except for the use of brief quotations in a book review.

ACKNOWLEDGEMENTS

An enormous thank you to Claire Jarrett, my editor, for challenging me and making me a better storyteller.

Thank you to Mayhem Cover Creations for the beautiful book cover.

And thank you to my readers, many of whom have also become friends. My gratitude is eternal.

1

RAVEN

Raven Cross was standing alone in a Georgia hotel room.

On the twin bed in front of her, there was an array of expensive camping equipment – her one-man tent, a mummy-style sleeping bag, a camp stove and compact cooking pot, her trekking poles, a pair of pink Spandex pants and a loose-fitting tank top, a pair of expensive trail-running shoes, several pairs of socks, a couple pounds of food packed neatly in a waterproof, bear-proof bag, and the slim hiking pack that she'd use to carry it all on her back for the next six months.

Additionally, there were a few dozen cardboard boxes in her parents' guest room back in Illinois – drop boxes containing all the food, section maps, clean socks and underwear Raven would need along the way, and there were a couple of maps spread across the hotel desk. She'd spent the last hour checking and re-checking her travel plans. Her family thought the idea was more than a little nuts, but Raven was ready for the journey.

She needed it.

She was just opening her food bag to double-check the meals that would sustain her during the first week of the trip when she heard a gentle knock on the door.

"Come in," she called, and her sister, Annabel, entered. She was just a few years younger than Raven – her fortieth birthday was earlier in the month and the whole family had ordered slices of cake from the hotel restaurant tonight as a belated celebration – but she looked decades younger than Raven's battle-worn, graying hair and premature wrinkles. "Hey, Anna."

"Hi," she said, coming in and closing the door again behind her. "What are you doing?"

"Just going over my supplies one last time," Raven said. Her parents and sister had accompanied her on the eleven-hour drive from Chicago to Gainesville, Georgia, today, and Raven knew that Annabel was still anxious about the whole thing.

"So this is all you need for six months on the Appalachian Trail, huh?" she asked as she came over to the bed to inspect Raven's equipment. She picked up a compact Swiss Army knife and flipped open the small blade with a frown.

Raven knew what she was thinking – that the trail was dangerous for a single woman to hike alone, and moreover, it was too much for a fragile cancer survivor like herself to handle. That was exactly why Raven *needed* to go on this journey, and she wasn't in the mood to be coddled on the night before she set out. She ignored Annabel's concerned look and pointed to the drop boxes stacked along the wall, saying, "This, and all the resupply boxes Mom and Dad are going to ship to me along the way."

It had taken her two whole weeks to calculate how much food she'd need and when, and another week to shop for all her equipment and food. She'd labeled each drop box with her name and the address of a post office located at strategic points along the 2,190-mile trail. There was half a year's worth of freeze-dried vegetables, dried fruit, trail mix, rice, and just-add-water pasta dishes in those boxes.

Raven had put sticky notes on the side of each box, telling her parents when to send each one to meet her at the right point on the trail, and all of it would require her to follow a finely orchestrated trail itinerary. That was not to mention the fact that she'd been lucky to take a semester-long sabbatical from her teaching job at the university, but she'd need to time her trip carefully to be back in time for the winter semester.

She took the Swiss Army knife out of Annabel's hand, closing it and setting it carefully back down on the bed with the rest of her supplies. Everything that went into her pack had been intentionally chosen and Anna had a habit of picking things up in one place and then setting them down somewhere else – she'd done it since they were kids, and since they were kids it had driven Raven up the wall.

With her hands empty, Annabel plopped down on

the other bed – hers for the night - and asked, "Raven, are you sure this trip is a good idea?"

Here it comes – the concerned look. After three years of trying to come to terms with her new identity as a breast cancer survivor, Raven knew the signs when someone was about to express sympathy for her battle, or worry over her physical capability.

Sure enough, Annabel's brow furrowed and she looked sick with worry.

Raven slumped down on the bed beside her, wrapping her arms around her sister's shoulders. Annabel lived all the way across the country in Seattle, and Raven knew she felt bad that she wasn't here when Raven and her parents were struggling through her treatment. Annabel still thought of Raven as sick and vulnerable, even though she'd been cancer-free for two years, because she'd been frozen in her mind at that ugly point in their lives.

That was one very big reason why she *needed* to conquer the Appalachian Trail – to prove that she *could*.

"It's not as dangerous as most people think," Raven said. "Did you know there have only been eleven murders on the Appalachian Trail since the 1970s? That's an insanely low crime rate – I'd have better odds on the AT than I do staying in Chicago for the same time period."

"I just can't stop thinking about you out there all by yourself," Annabel said, putting her head on Raven's shoulder.

"I won't be by myself," Raven tried to comfort her.

"Thousands of people hike the trail every year. A lot of them are solo hikers, and plenty of them are women. I'll be running into other hikers all the time, and it's not like I'm dropping off the face of the earth for the next six months. I'll call you every time I get to a trail town to pick up one of my drop boxes."

"Which you're going to hitchhike into," Annabel said. "Lord only knows what happens to female hitchhikers in the mountains…"

"Nothing happens to them," Raven said. "Look, I promise I won't hitchhike alone if you promise not to tell Mom that I'm planning to hitch rides."

That was one detail that Raven had left out when she was telling her parents about the trip. They'd been skeptical like Annabel at first, but when Raven explained why hiking the trail was so important to her, they made an effort to suppress their concerns and be supportive instead. Raven, in turn, had chosen to gloss over a couple of the more worrying details – she knew that she'd be fine, but after everything they'd gone through since her diagnosis just over three years ago, her mom had turned into a bit of a worrier.

"What about…" Annabel sighed and looked down at her lap, and Raven felt her dinner growing dense in her stomach. *Here it comes.* "What about your health?"

"No more of a concern than any other hiker's," Raven said confidently, straightening her posture for effect. "Tomorrow is my two-year anniversary and the perfect day to start a new adventure. Anna, I feel like I've been walking around with a flashing neon sign over my head that says *Breast Cancer Survivor*. That's me, but it's not *all* of me. I'm forty-five years old, in good health, I've got a good job and a wonderful, supportive family. I don't want to be defined by that label anymore."

"I know," Annabel said. "I just worry about you."

"And that's exactly why I need to go," Raven said. "Anna, listen to me. I'll be fine."

"Okay," her sister said. She still looked worried, but she did her best to put on a brave face. "I'm going to go see what Mom and Dad are up to."

"Probably raiding the mini-bar in their room," Raven joked. "You know how wild they get on vacation."

Annabel smirked, then said, "Come join us when you're ready. I don't get to visit very often and I'd like to hang out before you disappear for six months."

"I'm not disappearing," Raven reassured her. "But I'll be there in a few minutes."

2
KIT

Kit Davis was bored at her desk on a Friday afternoon.

She was bored a lot of the time at this job. It was a contract position working on a data entry project, and she worked much faster and more efficiently than the other people in her temporarily assigned department. That wasn't a very good strategy for a temp worker to have – she knew that the longer she could draw out this project, the longer she'd have a job at Baker and Price Accounting. But was it a job worth having?

There was almost an hour left in the work week and she'd run out of work to do just before lunch. She was waiting for her boss, Randall, to come up with another project for her, and in the meantime, she was playing Candy Crush on her phone and not bothering to look busy.

After all, it wasn't her fault she had nothing to do.

She worked fast and that was one of the things the temp agency liked about her.

What she liked about the agency – and about mindless data entry jobs like this one – was the fact that she was free to move on whenever she pleased. Being tied down had never suited her much. She'd tried it only once since she finished college almost a decade ago, and it had ended disastrously.

She was absorbed in her game – Level 147 was a bitch and a half – when Randall popped his nearly-bald head over the wall of her cubicle and said, "Kit, can you come with me?"

"Sure," she said with a smile. "Am I in trouble?"

Randall didn't laugh and Kit wondered if he was pissed about the Candy Crush. She slipped her phone into the back pocket of her work slacks, then followed him. They weaved through the maze of cubicles on the production floor, then down a hall that led to the administrative offices. Randall stopped outside the door to the Human Resources director's office, waving Kit in.

A humorless trip to HR on a Friday afternoon – Kit had worked enough temp jobs in the last five years to know where this was going, and now she knew why Randall hadn't bothered to give her a new assignment after lunch. Baker and Price Accounting was done with her.

Maybe the next temp job will be a little livelier, she thought as she went into the room and sat down in a small chair opposite the HR director's desk. She was pretty sure the woman's name was Melissa – it had been less than three months ago when she'd been in this room filling out her new hire paperwork, tax forms, and emergency contact information.

"Hi, Katherine," Melissa said with a practiced, mildly sympathetic smile.

"Kit," she corrected her. She'd always considered Katherine to be far too formal, and she certainly never felt like a girly Katie or a responsible Kathy. She settled on Kit in elementary school and never looked back.

"Of course," Melissa smiled.

Randall sat down in the empty chair beside Kit and she knit her brows. She'd been let go quite a few times since she started taking temp jobs and the bosses always left her at the door to HR. What was he doing?

Despite Randall's presence, the meeting went about as Kit expected. Melissa told her that she'd done all the work Baker and Price had for her and thanked her for her help. Kit zoned out toward the middle of Melissa's speech because she'd heard it so many times before, thinking instead about how she'd have to give the temp agency a call on Monday and pray for an interesting placement next time. Accounting never really got her blood pumping, although the closest she'd gotten to a ledger at this job was digitizing the company's old, pre-computer files.

Then Randall reached behind him and pushed the office door closed, regaining Kit's attention. *That was new*.

He looked at her with an abundance of concern in his big puppy dog eyes, then said, "Kit, it's been a pleasure working with you and I want to take this opportunity to give you a few pointers for your career, if I may."

Kit raised her eyebrows, then said, "Knock yourself out."

"You do good work," he said. "You're fast and highly accurate. If I had a position open on my team, I'd definitely consider extending you an offer for full-time employment, as I know you've been bumping around the temp job pool for some time."

"Thank you," Kit said. Not that she'd take it – she liked her freedom. But she felt a *but* coming and she glanced at Melissa, hoping to avoid it.

No such luck.

"*But*," Randall said. "I think you'll find that you're much more hirable if you take a bit more initiative. You don't always have to wait for me to tell you what to do."

Kit gave him a skeptical look and asked, "How can anyone take ownership of data entry? Either there's work to be done or there isn't."

Randall ignored this comment, which was too snarky to be considered professional. It was clear that he thought he was delivering nuggets of wisdom, things that had never crossed Kit's impressionable mind. She looked young – everyone told her she had a baby face – and that meant all sorts of people had the urge to take her under their wing and dispense advice, whether it was desired or not.

"Well, over the last couple of months I've observed you spending quite a lot of time at the water cooler, so to speak," Randall went on. "Coffee breaks, bathroom breaks, checking your phone – all that time adds up. There's a time to socialize at work, and that time is lunch."

"Didn't you just say I do good work and I'm fast?" Kit asked, struggling hard not to roll her eyes. This was one of the reasons she appreciated the transience of temp work – she couldn't imagine being stuck with a guy like Randall for an entire career. "Who cares if I take a break as long as the work gets done? Do you know how much eye strain is involved in staring at spreadsheets all day long?"

She crossed her arms defensively in front of her chest. It was cruel and unusual to be let go on account of her commendable efficiency, then lectured about her work ethic in the next breath. It was clear that Melissa wasn't going to come to her aid any time soon, so Kit just sat back in her chair and waited for Randall to finish.

"I'm just trying to help," he said. "I know from your resume that you've got a bachelor's degree in anthropology, and while I'm sure that's not the most marketable background in the world, you certainly seem bright enough to land a full-time job somewhere and stop working the temp circuit. I just hope you'll take what I've said to heart for the sake of your career."

"Thanks," Kit said grudgingly. She'd liked Randall prior to this moment, despite a few managerial quirks that were par for the course. Now, he thought he knew her and she didn't particularly want to look at him.

"Well," Melissa said, squirming slightly in her seat.

"Baker and Price thanks you for your help with the digitization project. Are you ready to wrap things up?"

"Yes, I am," Kit said, managing to regain her professional composure.

"I hope you understand, but it's company policy to escort you out of the building," Melissa said. "I'll call security to take you back to your cubicle so that you can collect your things."

"Don't worry about it," Kit said. "There's nothing there I need."

She couldn't wait to get out of this stifling building. Two more hours and her girlfriend, Sam, would be done with work, and the two of them could spend the whole weekend snuggling up on Sam's couch, watching B movies and forgetting about Kit's joblessness before she picked herself up by the bootstraps and started fresh on Monday.

Kit didn't even have much at her desk – two months was hardly enough time to start putting down roots. Thus, she could either let a security guard escort her to her desk and turn her into a spectacle for an entire company of strangers, or Kit could cut her losses and leave the contents of her desk behind. It was basically just a coffee mug and a picture of her and Sam visiting Chimney Rock that she'd had framed and given her on their six-month anniversary. Kit could print another, and buy a new frame.

She got up and Randall frowned.

"Come on, don't be like that," he said. "I'm just trying to help you."

"What makes you think I need help?" Kit asked, standing tall.

She opened the office door and Melissa picked up her phone receiver, probably alerting security just in case Kit decided to steal any corporate wall art on the way out of the building. From the corner of her eye, she could see Randall following her into the hall. He didn't pursue her, though, and she didn't look back as she went through the front doors and into the parking lot.

It was a brisk March afternoon and the wind whipped across the open parking lot. Kit shivered, realizing there was one more thing at her desk – her winter coat. It was fine. She could buy a new one of those, too. It wasn't worth the humiliation of going back.

She marched quickly to her truck, climbing into the driver's seat and turning on the heat as she fired up the ignition and headed for Sam's apartment to wait for her.

SAM'S CAR was already parked in its customary spot outside of her townhouse apartment when Kit got there. She checked the time – it was still not quite five o'clock – and, confused, she went inside. She couldn't wait to snuggle into Sam's arms and tell her all about the mean things Randall said to her. Sam was a nurturer and she'd make Kit feel better about it.

But when she opened the apartment door, Kit found Sam waiting on the couch, her posture somewhat tense and unnatural. She was still wearing the starched white button-up shirt and crisp A-line skirt that she'd adopted as her work uniform, but her low-heeled shoes were laying on the floor by the entrance and her eyes were red.

"Who died?" Kit asked, only half-joking.

"Sit down," Sam said, pointing to the loveseat that sat catty-corner to the couch rather than inviting Kit to sit down beside her. "We need to talk."

"What's wrong?" Kit asked, nervous butterflies forming in her stomach.

At work, she had known exactly what was coming as soon as Randall pointed her into the HR office, and it was becoming more clear by the moment what was about to happen here.

"Sit," Sam repeated, tucking an errant strand of long, dark hair behind her ear. She looked like she'd been crying, and Kit did as she was asked, sinking into the loveseat. Sam looked down at her hands, twisting anxiously in her lap. Then she said, "I don't really know how to say this."

Kit nodded.

Sam didn't need to say anymore. She knew a break-up talk when she heard it, whether from another temp job or from her girlfriend of nine months. Suddenly, Kit felt herself going cold – turning off. The rich, chestnut brown of Sam's hair seemed duller, and Kit was utterly unmoved by the faint dimple in her cheek that used to send a little jolt of desire through her every time it appeared.

She didn't need Sam, and she didn't need that job.

"You're breaking up with me," she said, sparing Sam the trouble.

Sam finally looked up, meeting Kit's eyes, and that was all the confirmation she needed. She was crying, her mascara beginning to run down her cheeks, and Kit thought in a removed, curious sort of way that this was a very bad day.

She was just opening her mouth to tell Sam she'd been let go at the accounting company when she said, "I'm sorry. It's just that you and I are at such different stages in our lives. We're in our thirties and you still act like you're in your early twenties most of the time. I've been trying to wait for you to be ready for commitment, moving in together, maybe even marriage down the line, but you're no different than the day I met you. You squirm every time I even *say* the M word – you did it just now."

"I'm sorry I'm not ready to rent the U-Haul," Kit said sarcastically. "You act like thirty-four is one or two birthdays away from the old age home. Forgive me if I've still got a lot more life to live."

When they'd first begun dating, Kit thought it was cute how grown-up Sam was, and she'd enjoyed playing house for a while. She slept over at Sam's apartment a few nights a week, and they'd do adult things like buying expensive groceries for romantic dinners at home, and double-dating with Sam's married friends, and weekend get-aways to cabins in the Blue Ridge Mountains nearby.

It stopped being fun when Sam started making it known that she wanted more, even though Kit had been very clear from the beginning that she had no more to give. At least, *she* thought she'd been clear. It was only a matter of time before they reached this very moment.

"I love you," Sam said. "I really do. But I think it's best for both of us if we take a break for a while until we can get on the same page about where we're headed."

"Until I can get on your page, you mean," Kit corrected. Why was everyone expecting *her* to be the one to change? Maybe she *liked* the way things were. "I got fired today."

The words came out before she could stop them. She knew it would only make Sam feel worse about this whole thing, but she'd said it anyway.

"You did?" Sam asked, concern in her voice. "What happened?"

Kit sighed. "Not fired, exactly. Laid off – I worked myself out of yet another temp job."

"Do you want to talk about it?" Sam asked.

"No," Kit said. "We're broken up. It's not your job to comfort me anymore."

"I still care about you, though," Sam said, and for the first time since she sat down, Kit felt a twinge of sadness.

She shoved it deep down in her gut and stood up, saying, "I better go. I think we've talked enough for one night."

"Okay," Sam said meekly, and for a moment, Kit wanted to go to her. She had a strong urge to fold Sam up in her arms and comfort her – promise her that she could be the person that everyone wanted her to be.

But that wasn't Kit.

That was Katie, or Katherine, or some other girl she didn't know.

So she went outside, shivering again, and climbed into her truck. She drove across town to her parents' house, where she'd moved back to her childhood bedroom about five years ago and hadn't yet found a good enough reason to move out. What she paid her parents in rent every month for the ten-by-ten-foot room would pay for a shabby studio apartment in Asheville, but the lack of a contract and the ability to get up and leave any time she wanted was priceless – even if Kit didn't actually go anywhere.

Now, though?

There was nothing keeping her here, and she thought she just might go.

3

RAVEN

Raven stood with her parents and sister at the southern approach to the Appalachian Trail. It was March 31st in Georgia, which turned out to be a significantly warmer day than March 31st in Chicago. Raven had her pack on her back – all twenty-five pounds of it - and both her mother and her sister had tears in their eyes.

They were making a valiant effort to hold them back, but there was no way Raven would set foot on the trail, pushing pause on her life for the next six months, without at least a few tears.

She'd cried enough in the last three years, though, and tears didn't come easily to her own eyes now. So she held her chin up and focused on technical details instead, telling her mother, "Don't forget to send my resupply boxes along. I shipped the first one myself before we left Illinois, but you'll need to send the second one at the end of this week to make sure it arrives on time."

"You've got everything you need, right?" her mom asked. "Food, maps, first aid supplies, the confirmation numbers for your motel bookings along the way?"

"It's all in the pack," Raven said. "Or else in the drop boxes back home. If I forgot anything, there will be grocery stores and outdoor shops along the way."

There was no way she'd forgotten anything, though. She'd done long hikes before – just never quite *this* long – and she knew what to pack. Plus, she'd inventoried all her supplies at least a half-dozen times in the weeks leading up to the trip. Any nervous energy she felt about her ability to conquer the Appalachian Mountains was immediately channeled into meticulously organizing her supplies.

Raven put her arm around her mom's shoulder, pulling her into a side hug, and then looked at her sister. Annabel had been quiet on the short drive from Gainesville to the starting point of the trail on Springer Mountain.

So had their dad, but then again, that was just his way. He stood beside Mom with one hand on her shoulder, providing silent comfort, and it reminded Raven of how he'd been the family's rock while she was undergoing surgery and the subsequent radiation treatment. He always complemented Mom's worrying and Annabel's big emotions, and he gave Raven the strength to be brave even when she felt like breaking.

"You guys going to survive without me?" she asked, laughing to break the tension.

"Call often," Annabel said. "Otherwise I'll worry."

"I can't call *too* often," Raven reminded her. "There are no power outlets on the mountain, so I have to conserve my phone battery as much as possible. I'll call you every time I go into a trail town to resupply."

That meant she'd be out of communication with her family - and the rest of the world, for that matter – for about five days at a time, all the way up the trail. She'd have cell reception at certain points along the trail, where there were no trees and lots of open sky, which was good in case of an emergency but she'd have to save her battery for when she needed it.

Raven talked to her parents every single day, and she called or texted her sister almost as often. She knew it might be lonely on the trail, but she was also looking forward to having the room to breathe the fresh mountain air and be on her own.

She needed to regain a little independence and a sense of herself.

"I better hit the trail," Raven said, glancing into the woods.

There was a big stone archway and a paved path leading into the park that would carry her to the southern terminus of the Appalachian Trail. A few other hikers had approached and disappeared into the park since Raven and her family arrived, and she was beginning to feel itchy to start her journey. Goodbyes were always hard and drawing them out only made things worse.

"I need to get going if I want to get to the first shelter by nightfall," she said, squeezing her mother into a tighter hug before letting her go and reaching for her sister.

Raven felt a few hot tears melting into the fabric of her shirt as Annabel cried quietly in her arms, and then she held her at arm's length and said, "I'm going to be fine, and you'll all be meeting me in Bangor before you know it."

Annabel nodded and Mom dug into her purse, pulling out her digital camera. "Let's get a picture of you standing at the entrance."

Raven struck a pose beneath the stone archway. The official beginning of the Appalachian Trail was about eight miles further up, marked by a bronze plaque of a hiker and bearing the inscription, *A footpath for those who seek fellowship with the Wilderness*. Raven would have to take her own photograph of that particular milestone, and from there until Maine, she would follow the white blazes painted on the trees to mark her journey.

She wondered how many other hikers had stood in this exact place and struck the same pose before her. She'd registered herself at the Trail Conservancy Center earlier in the day and she was now thru-hiker number 932 for the year.

Her mom put away the camera and Raven gave everyone another round of hugs, then said, "I'll call you when I get to Helen."

"Have fun, sweetie," her dad said as he encircled her in his large, protective arms.

She felt a lump form in her throat then, and when her mom told her she loved her, a few tears escaped down Raven's cheeks.

"I love you, too," she said, her voice cracking slightly. "I'll see you in six months, okay?"

Then she turned and walked through the archway, adjusting her pack on her back as the tears continued to fall down her cheeks. They didn't last long, as she breathed deeply of the mountain air and felt the sun on her face. With every step forward, she was shedding her old identity and becoming someone new – someone stronger, someone who could take a terrible event in her life and turn it into a beautiful new adventure.

RAVEN SPENT her first day on the trail enjoying the sounds and sights of nature – the birds chirping in the trees above her and the crunch of gravel beneath her feet as the paved portion of the trail gradually made way to the worn dirt path of the AT. She passed a few hikers and was passed by a few more, and even though she wasn't used to carrying twenty-five pounds on her back just yet, she'd never felt less burdened.

At the end of the day, she arrived at the Hawk Mountain Shelter, the first of many along the trail. Raven had covered an ambitious sixteen miles on her first day and tomorrow, her feet and thighs would be hurting. She'd done her best to break in her trail runners before she arrived on the mountain, and she'd done a few local hikes around the Chicago area to get back into the hiking form of her younger days, but there was nothing like the first day on a real mountain trail. She knew there would be aches and pains, and she welcomed them as proof that she was alive, she was here, and her body was capable.

Tomorrow, she'd do another thirteen miles. She'd mapped out the entire trip down to the day and she was planning on averaging twelve to fifteen miles a day all the way to the northern terminus on Mount Katahdin in Maine.

As she approached the shelter, which was nothing more than a large wooden platform, open on one side and covered with a roof to protect hikers from the elements, she noticed that there was already quite a party going on. There were at least a dozen hikers setting up tents outside of the platform or cooking their dinners over camp stoves, and a trio of young men were sitting atop a picnic table with a bulging cooler bag between them.

"Incoming!" one of them called when he spotted Raven. He seemed to be in his early twenties, and at first glance, Raven wouldn't have taken him for a serious hiker. He wore a cotton tie-dyed t-shirt, his blonde hair was long and shaggy, and he pushed off the picnic table to join Raven as she reached the edge of camp. "Another thru-hiker?"

"Yeah," she said, looking over his shoulder as his friends watched their exchange. If she were younger and more naïve, she might be worried that this kid was here to hit on her, but Raven was good at giving off the *not interested* vibe – particularly to men, although in the last couple of years since her surgery, she'd shut herself off to women as well.

"Where are you from?" the kid asked.

"Illinois," she answered. He led her over to the picnic table and she followed because by now she was looking for an excuse to take off her pack. The straps were chafing her sides and she knew that was something she'd get used to over the next two-thousand miles, but for now she could use a break. "What about you?"

"Jersey," the kid said. He was practically bouncing back to the table, full of youthful exuberance that would probably be sufficient all on its own to get him up the trail. As Raven let her pack fall on the bench of the picnic table, he asked, "What's your name?"

"Raven," she said, extending her hand to him. Instead of shaking it, he reached into the cooler bag and pulled out a cold can of beer, slapping it into her palm with a grin.

"I'm Dodger," he said. "And this is my band of Merry Men."

One of the other guys rolled his eyes as he held out his hand to Raven, turning to Dodger to say, "I told you that you have it all mixed up. The Artful Dodger is Dickens. The Merry Men are from Robin Hood, and in any case, it makes you sound pretentious."

"How can it be pretentious if it's wrong?" Dodger asked with a gleeful smile, cracking open a new beer of his own.

Raven just laughed, and the other two introduced themselves. The one who knew his classic literature called himself Eagle Scout, and the third guy – who was already at least two sheets to the wind – said his name was Patrick.

"I don't have a trail name yet," he explained. "This is my first hike."

"Oh. Yeah, I don't have one, either," Raven said.

"Well, you can't name yourself," Dodger said. "It's a rule. We could give you a trail name if you want."

"Umm, maybe," Raven said, hedging. She wondered what kind of name a bunch of kids like this would give her. She opened her beer and took a long sip. It was cool and tasted better than any beer she'd had in recent memory, simply because of how refreshing it was after a long day of hiking in the Georgia sun. "Are you guys doing the whole trail?"

"We're going to try," Eagle Scout said. He sounded skeptical and Raven couldn't blame him.

"Me too. Well, thanks for the beer," she said, slinging her pack over one shoulder. "I better set up my tent before nightfall. I'll talk to you later, okay?"

The shelter was already full with packs and sleeping bags, but that was okay. Raven was looking forward to the calm solitude of her little one-man tent. While she set it up, she watched the people around her. There were hikers of all ages, some looking like they were at the peak of their physical prowess and others who would shed fat stores along with other unnecessary things along the trail. Some of them stuck close to each other – probably hiking in pairs or groups like Dodger and his men – and there were a couple other solo hikers keeping to themselves like Raven.

A few more hikers trickled in and Dodger greeted each of them with a cold beer – their first taste of trail magic on the long journey ahead. That cooler bag must have been hell to lug all the way up here, but the beer was just what Raven needed to unwind at the end of her first day's hike.

THE NEXT COUPLE of days went by much faster than Raven expected. The days began to blend together in a good way, and her feet and thighs grew accustomed to the drastic increase in physical activity.

Raven learned to appreciate every delicious bite of the food that sustained her body, as well as every beautiful view and moment of solitude along the way. She passed a lot of other hikers – the beginning of the trail was full of bright-eyed people at the beginnings of their own individual journeys. Some of them told her their stories, like the newlywed couple who were section hiking during their honeymoon, and the retired Marine who was using the trail to decompress after coming home from a tour.

She hiked for a day with Dodger and his crew and they told her that they'd all graduated from Kean University the previous spring and had agreed to take a gap year together before starting their careers. The Appalachian Trail was their last hurrah before responsible adulthood, and Raven could tell they intended to make the most of the journey.

"What about you?" Patrick asked after Eagle Scout finished explaining their itinerary to Raven. He'd earned the trail name *Break Time* after his first couple of days, and after a couple of hours of leisurely hiking with this group, it wasn't hard to figure out the reason. "Why are you out here?"

"Well, I was sitting alone in my apartment one day and there just wasn't a single good show on TV," Raven said. She'd learned after being asked this question by almost everyone she met that this response was liable to get a laugh, and it worked on the guys. She followed it up quickly with a few questions about what kind of work they were all going into when they finished the trail, and it worked like a charm – they didn't pry any further.

Raven hated the idea of bringing her vulnerable, battle-worn identity with her on the trail. If she went around telling everyone the truth – that her whole family still expected her to break at the slightest stress and that she hadn't felt like a woman since the doctor first removed the bandages on her chest to reveal her scarred and slightly deflated right breast – she might as well not even bother with this trip. So she made jokes and changed the subject, and that seemed to be working just fine.

She sat with the guys around a crackling campfire that night and they roasted a pack of marshmallows that Eagle Scout had brought, insisting that they get eaten before they turned into melty taffy in his pack. Raven discovered quickly that Dodger reveled in being the center of attention, and he regaled them with stories from his fraternity days. They were nothing new to Eagle

Scout and Break Time – they were *in* the stories – but Raven found them quite amusing.

"You have not lived until you've heard the high-pitched squeal of a grown man who is mid-coitus only to have an eight-pound iguana drop from the top bunk onto his back," Dodger said, slapping his thigh as tears streamed down his cheeks.

"Yeah, and whose iguana was it?" Eagle Scout asked.

"Mine, of course," Dodger said proudly. "I still don't know how she kept getting out of her enclosure."

"I'm not convinced it was an accident," Break Time accused, looking a little saltier than necessary until Raven began to suspect that he was the fraternity brother from the story.

She didn't get a chance to inquire, though, because Dodger abruptly turned to her and said, "I've got it."

"What?"

"Your trail name," he said. "Lone Wolf."

Raven wrinkled her nose. "Really?"

"Yeah," Dodger said confidently. "It's perfect."

"It sounds so antisocial," she objected.

"You like to hike by yourself, you *always* sleep in your tent instead of in the shelter with everyone else, and I've yet to hear a single entertaining campfire story from you," Dodger said. "You're a lone wolf if I ever saw one."

"So I'm not a team player unless I share an embarrassing sex story?" she asked.

"Doesn't have to be yours," Eagle Scout pointed out, poking fun at Dodger.

Raven's cheeks colored for a moment and she felt

foolish that a group of twenty-something kids had the ability to make her feel embarrassed. But she wasn't about to reveal her intimate moments, or her sexuality for that matter, for their amusement. She'd have to reach pretty far back in her memory for that, anyway.

"Fine," she said, reaching for another marshmallow to toast. "Lone Wolf it is."

RAVEN'S first trip into a trail town was at the end of the week. She hitched a ride into Helen, Georgia, which was a surprisingly colorful town. The shops along the main drag were all styled in Bavarian architecture with colorful paint and lots of greenery. It felt surreal to come down from the mountain and step into another world like that.

Raven went to the post office to pick up her first drop box, pausing outside to swap out the section map and load her next week's worth of food supplies into her pack. Some hikers chose to forego drop boxes, instead relying on carefully orchestrated visits to trail town grocery stores to resupply, but the food was often overpriced and the selection was unreliable. Unknowns weren't exactly Raven's style, and she'd removed as many variables from her journey as she could. She liked knowing how many miles she'd be hiking every day, and what would be waiting for her in her resupply boxes along the way.

She disposed of the empty cardboard box in a nearby trash can, then dug her phone out of her pack to call home.

While she waited for the call to connect, Raven wandered down the street to explore the whimsically decorated town. She was just wandering into Betty's Country Store when her mother picked up.

"Raven!" she exclaimed. "I've been waiting by the phone all day. How are you?"

"I'm good, Mom," Raven laughed. "Everything's good. How about you?"

"I'm just the same as always," her mother said dismissively, then the phone went staticky for a second as she covered the receiver and called out, "Alan, Raven's on the phone!"

"How are you and Dad doing as empty-nesters once again?" Raven asked while she waited for her Dad to join them. Annabel had flown from Seattle to spend a few days with the family before Raven started her journey, and Raven had spent almost a year living in her childhood bedroom after she'd gotten sick. The circumstances weren't happy ones, but she knew how much her parents enjoyed having the two of them back home, even for short stretches.

"We're doing well," her mom said, then chastised, "but I don't want to talk about us right now. You're the one on an adventure! Oh, here's Dad. I'm putting you on speakerphone, Raven."

"Hey Daddy," Raven said. She felt a lump forming in her throat, and to chase it away, she said, "Actually, I go by Lone Wolf now."

She wandered through the tight aisles of Betty's while she explained the concept of trail names to her parents. The store was just as old-fashioned and quaint as the rest of the town, with big barrels full of bulk goods dominating the space, plus a wall of locally-produced jellies, mouth-watering baked goods, and a small meat counter.

What really drew Raven's attention, though, was the produce section. She'd never craved fresh fruits and vegetables as much as she did now that her access to them was so limited. She examined a tantalizing display of Georgia peaches while she allayed her mother's fears about her new nickname.

"You're not too isolated out there, are you?"

"No," Raven assured her. "It's not like that. There are plenty of other hikers and I pass people all the time. I've even made a couple of friends – they're the ones who gave me the trail name."

She wasn't quite sure she'd call Dodger and his Merry Men friends in real life – not with the age difference, or the amusing frat guy attitudes. But on the trail, they were perfectly fine companions.

She chose a couple of peaches – she'd have to eat them tonight or else they'd bruise and rot quickly in the cramped quarters of her pack. Then to make sure her parents didn't leave the call worrying about her, Raven told them about some of the best things she'd encountered so far on her journey.

"The views are absolutely phenomenal," she said. "Nothing like the parks around Chicago. It's so freeing to just let go of everything and simply hike. Just this morning, I was on top of Tray Mountain, and the horizon just goes on forever there. It's the very definition of rolling hills and you can just tell from standing there that the view has inspired countless paintings."

"I'm glad you're having a good time," her mom said as Raven wandered over to the bakery and considered getting herself something sweet for dessert. "Just remember that if it stops being fun, or if you get tired, we'll come right down and pick you up."

If you get tired. Raven knew what that meant – they were still worried about her, still not confident that her body was strong enough to carry her on this journey. Well, they were wrong.

"Thank you," she said graciously. "But I'm in this for the long haul. I need to call Anna now and reassure her that I'm not dead. I'll call you again in about a week, okay?"

"Okay, dear," her mom said. "We love you."

"Love you, kiddo," her dad said.

"I love you guys, too," Raven answered. "Don't forget my drop box, okay?"

She hung up, wondering if she was going to feel like crying every single time she called her family from here until Mount Katahdin. Raven didn't feel homesick until she heard their voices, and then it suddenly seemed impossible that she wouldn't see any of them for half a year.

She took her peaches to the cashier, then went outside and found an outlet where she could plug in her phone to keep it charged up while she called Annabel.

4

KIT

Kit began her hike at Max Patch Mountain in North Carolina. It was just an hour's Uber drive from Asheville and she'd been staring at those mountains for most of her life. She always loved the romanticism of disconnecting and losing herself on the Appalachian Trail, and ever since the day she'd snarkily begun calling The Worst Day of My Life, a single thought had been recurring in her mind again and again.

Why not now?

So she emptied her savings account at the outdoor shop, stocking up on hiking gear, and set out on a new adventure because there was nothing tying her to Asheville and no one depending on her for anything. She was thirty-four years old and if she had done what everyone kept hounding her to do – settle down, grow up, put down roots – she might not have this beautiful opportunity now.

Who else could put their life on hold on a whim to

disappear into the wilderness? This was what life was all about, and the reason she so stubbornly refused to conform to everyone else's expectations for her.

At least, that's what she'd been thinking when she first set foot on the trail that morning, bright-eyed and bushy-tailed. But by the time the sun was beginning to sink over the mountain ridges, she was feeling a little less enthusiastic.

The hiking boots she'd chosen rubbed blisters on her toes, and what felt like a reasonable amount of weight in her pack this morning had turned into an almost intolerable burden after a few hours on the trail. It was much more rustic than she'd expected, just uneven dirt paths that wound through the forest with jagged rocks poking her soles and fallen limbs to climb over.

Kit hadn't given much thought to the weight of her supplies when she bought all her gear, instead focusing on price and size so that she could fit as much as she thought she'd need inside her small pack. She realized that was a mistake now – that, or all the other hikers who passed her during the day were actually part pack mule and that explained her struggles.

She was lucky to meet up with a father and son pair in the late afternoon. He noticed how much she was fidgeting with the weight of her pack and offered to adjust the straps for her. That helped a bit, but it was even more useful when the kid invited her to hike with them. It gave her something to focus on besides the pain in her shoes.

"My name's Alec," he said. "My dad and me are

going to hike all the way to Clingman's Dome. Where are you hiking?"

"I don't know yet," Kit said. "I just started today, and I'm not really big into the whole planning thing. I'll probably just hike until I feel like stopping."

"Well, you're welcome to tag along with us as long as you like," Alec's dad said. Kit found out through the course of the conversation that his name was Dave, Alec was eight years old, and working on his hiking merit badge for the Boy Scouts.

"Do you come out here often?" she asked.

"As much as I can," Dave said. "When you've got a playground like this in your back yard, it's a shame not to use it. I didn't have a hard time convincing Alec of that, but my wife on the other hand..."

Kit laughed and conceded, "I've never done this before. I mean, I've gone camping with friends and done a few day hikes here and there. But nothing like the AT."

"Did you do any research before you came out here?" Dave asked, frowning.

Oh boy, Kit thought. Here came another father figure expressing concern.

"Not really," she said with a shrug. "I figured out what kind of equipment I'd need and I got a map of the trail. Other than that, I'm planning to wing it. I figure if I get in over my head or it's not fun, I'll just hitch a ride into some little town along the way and go home."

"Well, be careful," Dave said. "Plan out your food supplies and when you're going to refill your canteen, or else you'll find yourself eating leaves and twigs."

Alec crumbled into a fit of laughter at this idea, and Kit felt a twinge of nervousness for the first time since she'd set foot on the trail. Maybe she *should* have done a little more research before she went off half-cocked into the mountains.

She pushed the idea aside, though. She was here now, and there was nothing she could do about it at this point. She and Dave spent the rest of the late afternoon listening to Alec point out chipmunks and interesting-looking rocks and views along the trail, skipping ahead of them with the boundless energy of a child, and just as night began to fall, they reached the Fontana Dam Shelter where they'd settle in for the night.

There were four other hikers already there – three guys a little younger than Kit and a slightly older woman who sat a little way off from them, heating rice on her camp stove. When the guys spotted the new arrivals, one of them called, "Welcome to the Fontana Hilton!"

Kit smiled, then went over to a pair of stone benches that sat on either side of a fire pit where the guys were gathered. She shrugged off her pack and collapsed onto the bench with an exaggerated sigh. The woman looked up at her, her dark eyes surprisingly fiery, and Kit couldn't tell if she was silently judging her theatrics or just looking at the newcomer out of curiosity.

"Where you from?" the shaggy-haired guy who had greeted them asked from the other stone bench.

"Oh, we're not together," Kit clarified while Dave and Alec unloaded their own packs and sat down in the grass. "We just met this afternoon. I'm from Asheville."

"And we're on the other side of the mountain – Knoxville," Dave said. He put out his hand to shake with the guy, and the other two as well. The woman looked up from her camp stove again, smiling in a curiously reserved way, and she shook his hand as well.

Kit was intrigued by her. She had a subtle kind of beauty, despite a few graying hairs in her nearly black mane, and Kit was drawn in a carnal way to the equally subtle hints of curves beneath her baggy shirt that hung low over her spandex pants, but that wasn't it. The energy she was giving off was not something Kit expected to encounter beneath the wide-open sky, and she wanted to know more about her.

"I'm Dodger," the guy said, taking back Kit's attention. "This is Break Time, Eagle Scout, and that's Lone Wolf."

Lone Wolf. Well, that's suiting.

"We're from New Jersey originally," the guy called Eagle Scout said. "Are you all section hikers or thru-hikers?"

"Section, definitely," Dave said with a laugh, ruffling his son's hair. "This one has to be back in school on Monday."

"I guess I'm a section hiker," Kit said. "I haven't decided yet."

Dodger laughed loudly at this, and Lone Wolf's eyes went wide. Now *that* was a judgmental look.

Dave and Alec excused themselves to go use the showers – a rare treat on the trail, from what Kit heard –

and Dodger came over to Kit's bench, sliding next to her and asking, "So, you got a name?"

Kit tried not to roll her eyes because she was pretty sure he was hitting on her. Apparently, her partially shaved hair and the baggy cargo shorts she was wearing weren't enough to signal her disinterest, but curiously, she noticed Lone Wolf watching their interaction with more interest than she'd shown in the conversation previously.

Kit smiled and held out her hand, keeping her arm rigid to force a little distance between her and Dodger, then said, "Kit Ballard. Nice to meet you."

"No trail name?" he asked, not missing a beat.

"Not yet," she said. "I'm pretty new to all this."

"We could call you Forrest Gump," Break Time offered. He affected a Tom Hanks voice to match the movie as he said, "I just felt like hiking."

Kit smirked, then said, "I don't know. I'll think about it."

"You don't get to *choose* your trail name," Dodger said. "It's assigned to you. That's tradition."

Kit just shrugged and said, "Tradition is overrated. I've got to use the latrine."

"It's that way," Eagle Scout said, pointing in the direction that Dave and Alec had gone.

She left her pack on the ground and went to find the bathroom – a much nicer one than the glorified holes in the ground she knew she'd be finding at other points on the trail. When she came back to the campsite, Dodger and the other guys were in the big wooden shelter, laying out their sleeping bags on the bunked platforms within, and Lone Wolf was still sitting by the fire, finishing the last of her meal.

Kit went over to her, ready to dig a little deeper into this intriguingly closed off woman. She asked, "Can I sit with you?"

"I don't own the fire," Lone Wolf said. Then she added, "Go ahead."

"What's for dinner?" Kit asked, nodding to the cooking pot in her hand.

"Chicken-flavored rice," she said, surprising Kit by loosening up a little bit. "It's like no chicken I've ever tasted before but I love it, even more now that I work so hard for all my meals every day."

Kit crawled around the edge of the fire and grabbed her pack, then brought it back over to where Lone Wolf sat with her back against the edge of the stone bench. She said, "I've got a Snickers bar and a packet of ramen noodles."

Lone Wolf laughed, a few fine wrinkles appearing around her mouth. They enhanced her beauty and Kit watched her openly. "I'm willing to bet you've got the melted *remains* of a Snickers bar."

Kit smiled, then dug her food out of her pack. She opened the Snickers bar and nodded, then showed Lone Wolf the melty remains. "You're right. Oh well, beginner's mistake. It'll still taste good."

She licked melted chocolate from the inside of the wrapper, and out of the corner of her eye, she saw that Lone Wolf's eyes were on her tongue. *Interesting.*

"So what's your real name?" Kit asked after a minute. "Or am I not supposed to ask that?"

"I have no idea," the woman said. "It's Raven."

"Beautiful," Kit said before she could help herself. She couldn't have chosen a better name for her – Raven's dark, silky hair and creamy skin matched it perfectly.

"It's a little gothic," Raven said, brushing off the compliment and blushing slightly. "My parents are both literature professors and they're big Poe fans. You'll never guess my sister's name."

"Nevermore?" Kit asked.

Raven laughed and Kit couldn't tear her eyes off her mouth if she tried. "No, Annabel – as in, *It was many and many a year ago, in a kingdom by the sea...*"

"Sorry," Kit said. "I was an anthropology major so you know I didn't learn anything useful in college."

Raven laughed again. Kit wondered how many more times she could make her do that tonight because it was a wonderful sight to behold. She pulled her camp stove out of her pack after she finished with the Snickers bar and used her canteen water to cook the ramen.

While she did that, Raven asked, "Did you really come out here without a plan?"

"Yeah," Kit said. She looked over her shoulder at Raven and her eyes had gone a little wide again. She laughed and said, "That scares you, doesn't it?"

"I just don't know how anyone could set out on a journey like this without knowing where they're going," Raven said.

"I'm going north," Kit said. There was just one path

to follow, and in her mind, there were no unanswered questions about that. She smiled and asked, "Let me guess – you're the kind of person who can't go on vacation without a printed itinerary."

"I can," Raven said, then after a pause, she added, "I just not to."

Kit laughed again. Then as she took the noodles off her stove and waited for them to cool, she asked, "So where are you from?"

"Chicago," Raven said. "I've been on the trail almost three weeks now and I'm going to do the entire thing."

"I don't doubt that," Kit answered.

Then Dave and Alec came back to the campsite, sitting together on the other stone bench. They introduced themselves to Raven and Dave taught Alec how to light his camp stove, and in the shelter, Kit could hear Dodger and his friends laughing and joking with each other.

She leaned back, putting her hands behind her head and letting her head rest on the bench so that she could look up at the stars. Her aches and pains were gone for now, although she was sure they'd be back with a vengeance tomorrow morning when it was time to start walking again. In the moment, though, she felt a profound sense of peace settling over her.

This was exactly where she needed to be, and these were the people she needed to be with. The universe had a way of providing moments like this.

After a minute or two, she lifted her head again and

looked at Raven. She said on a whim, "I think *you* should pick my trail name."

"Me?" Raven asked, surprised. "I barely know you."

"You'll just have to get to know me better, then," Kit said, feeling bold. She smiled and put her head back on the bench, looking at the stars again. "Let me know when you think of it."

5

RAVEN

When Raven woke up the next morning, it was early and everyone else was still asleep. Kit and the guys had chosen to lay out their sleeping bags in the shelter, while Dave and his son shared a two-man tent that looked luxuriously large compared to Raven's little one.

She'd thought about joining everyone else in the shelter last night, but she knew from experience that Break Time was a snorer and she had a long day of hiking ahead of her today. She needed her sleep, so she'd ended up in her tent as usual.

She crawled out of it now, throwing her arms wide in a deep stretch as she inhaled the crisp morning air. The campfire smoldered nearby, the last few embers burning themselves out, and the camp felt peaceful with all its other occupants sleeping soundly.

Raven went down to the showers and washed up in solitude, then filled her canteen before going back to the campsite. Everyone was still asleep as she passed the shelter, slowing as she noticed Kit sleeping soundly on the bottom platform. The longer strands of her dusty blonde hair hung in chaotic tendrils over her forehead, obscuring her eyes, and Raven allowed herself to be hypnotized for a moment by the steady rise and fall of her chest.

The girl was something else. Raven found herself both fascinated and horrified by her approach to the trail, and she shook her head as she tiptoed back over to her tent. She dismantled it quietly – she could do it with her eyes closed at this point – and packed up her things.

She grabbed a protein bar from her food bag for breakfast, deciding to eat it while she hiked, and as she walked away from the Fontana Dam Shelter, she found herself hoping that this wouldn't be the last she saw of Kit. It was pretty common to run into the same hikers again and again on the trail – Raven had wound up camping with Dodger, Break Time and Eagle Scout quite a few times – but it was hard to say how long a girl like Kit would last in the mountains.

Raven hadn't given her a trail name yet. Nothing came to her while they sat around the fire last night, and the idea of naming a stranger had been, frankly, overwhelming. As she started her hike for the day, Raven hoped that unfinished business would ensure a repeat encounter.

IT TURNED out to be several days before she next met Kit. She wasn't at the campsite that Raven chose that night, or the following day, and just when she was beginning to worry that she'd lost her – or that Kit had realized she was in over her head out here and thrown in the towel – Raven found her unexpectedly.

She was in Gatlinburg, Tennessee, picking up one of her resupply boxes. She'd just finished talking to her parents and Annabel, and decided to spend the afternoon wandering down the long road full of shops, restaurants, bars and tourists. Quite a few of them were carrying around enormous ice cream cones that made Raven's mouth water, and she'd made it her mission to locate the shop that sold them and buy the most absurdly indulgent cone she could create.

Raven was one of the only hikers in town, feeling conspicuous with her pack on her back and wearing the same pink spandex shorts and baggy tank top that she'd had since Springer Mountain.

Everyone else in this town was dressed nicely, looked freshly showered and pampered by all the modern conveniences of hotel rooms and soft beds.

Everyone except one.

Raven noticed a girl with short blonde hair on the other side of the street. Her back was turned and she had her pack resting on a wooden bench, struggling to fit a couple of grocery bags into it while tourists wandered past her, oblivious.

Raven smiled, then jogged across the street as soon as there was a lull in traffic. Kit might not have a *clue* when it came to hiking the Appalachian Trail, but Raven already knew she was good for a little entertainment, and she was too curious not to ask what exactly she was doing.

"Hey," she said, making Kit jump slightly as she came up behind her. "Got a trail name yet, or are you still just Kit?"

She smiled – happy to see Raven – and then her lips turned into a playful smirk as she said, "Not unless you thought of one for me."

"Still thinking," Raven said. She unshouldered her own pack and set it on the bench next to Kit's, then asked, "What on earth are you doing?"

The two plastic grocery bags on the bench between them were packed full and even from across the street Raven could see that they were *never* going to fit into Kit's streamlined hiking pack.

"Trail magic," Kit said, a twinkle in her brilliant blue eyes. She untied the knot from one of the bags, holding it open for Raven to look inside. The bag was filled with every type of candy she could imagine, and Raven felt an unexpected tingle at how close Kit's voice was when she asked, "What do you think? Is it a winner?"

Raven straightened up, making a little more space between them again, and wondered what had come over her. Kit was really cute, and based on their interaction at the Fontana Dam Shelter the other night, there was a higher than average chance that she might reciprocate the feeling. But she was so young and wild, Raven couldn't even comprehend the steps it would take to build up the courage to make a move.

She hadn't done anything like that in years, since before she'd gotten sick.

"It's a winner," Raven said, dismissing the thought and turning her attention back to Kit's bounty. "I know my sweet tooth has gone crazy ever since I got on the trail, and Dodger and his friends suck down roasted marshmallows like they're going out of style. There must be something chemical about a need for carbohydrates, or a desire for more interesting oral stimulation after endless rice and pasta dishes."

Her cheeks colored as she said *oral stimulation,* and she hoped that Kit didn't notice. Not that Kit seemed like the type of person who would shy away from a double entendre, but of all the old hang-ups Raven was trying to shed on this journey, she wasn't quite ready to tackle that one just yet.

"The thing is, I think I may have gone a little overboard," Kit said with a frown. She'd managed to cram the second bag of candy about halfway into her pack, but that was as far as she'd gotten.

Raven laughed and agreed with her. "You're never going to get both bags inside your pack. We could tie them to the outside, but the candy might melt."

"I tried to pick stuff that wouldn't melt," Kit said, pointing out the contents of the open bag. "Starburst, gummy bears, Twizzlers, jelly beans..."

"Smart," Raven said.

"Well, don't sound so surprised," Kit teased her. Raven apologized, but Kit brushed it off. "Help me tie the bags on? If I felt like a pack mule before, I'm *really* going to feel like one now."

She pulled the shopping bag out of her pack and zipped it up, then they tied one of the bags to the strap of Kit's pack. She put it on to test it out and said, "Oof! That really adds weight. I'm beginning to regret my random act of kindness."

"Don't do that," Raven said. "Everyone's going to love this. Here – I can carry the other bag until we get back on the trail, as long as you don't mind hanging out with me for the afternoon."

"Hanging out with Lone Wolf?" Kit asked. "Of course I don't mind. I've been *dying* to do just that."

Now Raven did blush visibly. *Really?* She kept her eyes on her task as she tied on the bag, and asked, "Why's that?"

"You're mysterious," Kit said. "I like that."

Raven could feel the heat between them – or was it the sun beating down on her? She could feel Kit's eyes on her and she kept her eyes averted down the street as she reshouldered her pack.

"Thanks for your help," Kit said. "Can I buy you a beer for your trouble?"

"How about one of those ice cream cones instead?" Raven asked, nodding to a group of teenagers coming up the sidewalk toward them, each one with a fist-sized ice cream cone that looked like heaven on earth to Raven.

"It's a deal," Kit answered.

They got their ice cream cones, eating them as slowly as they could afford to as the ice cream melted down the outside of the waffle cones, and spent another half an hour wandering lazily around Gatlinburg. Then they found a family passing through on their way to a rented cabin in the Smoky Mountains who were willing to give them a ride back to the trail.

There were about half a dozen hikers at the next shelter along the way at Newfound Gap, and Kit turned Raven around so she could untie the shopping bag from the bottom of her pack. Raven flinched slightly when Kit's hand touched her shoulder, but she didn't have time to focus on that incongruent reaction.

Instead, she watched as Kit proudly distributed her trail magic – a little unexpected gift that was made all the more special when it came at the exact moment when it was needed. Everyone dug in, picking out their favorites and moaning with delight as they chowed down on treats that they hadn't even realized they were longing for until that moment.

Then Kit came over and took Raven's hand, surprising her again and pulling her over to the gathered crowd. She shrugged off her pack and added the contents of the second shopping bag to the pile, and then they all sat around the giant heap of candy, indulging themselves.

Raven picked out a couple pieces of salt water taffy – her favorite type of candy – and said, "It's too bad Dodger and his crew aren't here. They'd be all over this."

"I hiked with them all day yesterday. They decided to yellow blaze this section of the trail," Kit said. "Eagle Scout wasn't too happy about driving instead of hiking, but Dodger kept saying 'quality is better than quantity,' and I think Break Time was inclined to agree."

Raven laughed, then said, "Well, I'm sure we'll catch up to them again at some point."

The group ate until they all had stomach aches, then hung the rest of the candy in a bear bag in the trees before bed. Kit wrote a note in the shelter log so that tomorrow's hikers could help themselves to the rest of the candy, and then they all turned in for the night. For the first time, Raven laid out her sleeping bag self-consciously beside Kit's in the shelter and slept soundly beneath the stars.

6
KIT

The sun was just beginning to rise when Kit heard a faint rustling noise that stirred her out of sleep. She opened her eyes and saw the world upside down. She'd rolled onto her back in a fit of sugar-induced dreaming and her head was now hanging over the edge of the shelter.

She winced – the pressure of the hard, wooden platform against her head had produced a mild headache and her sleeping bag didn't offer much in the way of padding. She'd noticed on her first night that a lot of other hikers carried inflatable or foam mattress pads – something she'd overlooked during her pre-hike shopping trip and which no doubt made the nights more comfortable.

Fortunately, she was still young and she could shake off the aches and pains in the first couple of miles on the trail each day. She'd even started to build up calluses where her hiking boots rubbed her ankles and was getting used to the weight of her pack.

She rolled onto her stomach and the pressure from her head dissipated. Yawning wide, she looked around the campsite and found the source of the rustling sound that had awakened her. Raven was standing a few feet away, rolling up her sleeping bag and stuffing it into her pack.

"What are you doing?" Kit whispered to her.

Raven looked up, surprised, and then she smiled at Kit. "Your hair looks ridiculous right now."

Kit put her hand to her hair. She hadn't been able to wash it in a couple of days and now it was standing up in a bunch of different directions. Rather than trying to smooth it down, she ruffled it up even further, then gave Raven a challenging grin.

"Much better," Raven chuckled.

"Why are you up so early?" Kit asked.

"Well, I hear there's this big, long trail around here," Raven said. "It goes all the way from Georgia to Maine, and some people spend *months* hiking it. I figured I'd have a go at it."

Kit laughed and yawned again, snuggling into her sleeping bag. The summer heat was coming, but for now, it was still a little chilly this early in the morning. "Itineraries are for suckers. You should relax a little."

"I can't," Raven said. "I have to make good time so I can be back in Chicago for the start of the fall semester."

"Do you teach?" Kit asked. She swung her legs over the edge of the platform, staying tucked cozily inside her sleeping bag as she wiped the sleep from her eyes.

"Yeah, microeconomics," Raven said. "What about

you? Do you have a job waiting for you back in North Carolina?"

"Nope," Kit said. "I'm free as a bird."

"Well, no wonder you don't care about keeping to a schedule," Raven said.

"Shut up," someone barked from within the shelter, grumpy at having been woken.

Kit whispered an apology, then climbed out of her sleeping bag and went over to stand beside Raven so they wouldn't have to talk so loudly. She whispered, "What's on the agenda today?"

"Clingman's Dome," Raven said. "It's the highest point on the entire Appalachian Trail."

"Oh, cool," Kit said. "Dave and Alec were heading there – wonder if they're ahead or behind us."

"I haven't seen them since the night we met," Raven whispered. "I doubt Alec can do as many miles in a day as I do, though. They must be behind us."

"Can I tag along with you?" Kit asked. She wondered if Lone Wolf would take exception to that, and whether she'd say so if she did.

Raven stood, shouldering her pack and pulling out her retractable trekking poles – another thing almost everyone Kit met had, but which she'd neglected to buy for herself. Raven looked her up and down, sizing her up in a way Kit did not mind at all, then she whispered with a sly smile, "You're welcome if you think you can keep up. Get your stuff – I want to get there early so we don't have to climb the Dome at the hottest part of the day."

Kit considered for a moment whether she should take

exception to Raven's concern that she wasn't up for the task, but instead, she obediently did as Raven asked. She gathered her things from the shelter as quietly as she could and they both filled their canteens, then set off on their day's journey.

The path was narrow for most of the morning, Kit trailing behind Raven and looking enviously at her trekking poles – they certainly weren't the most interesting part of the view back there, but they did provide a conversation piece.

"Do those poles make your pack feel lighter while you're walking?" Kit asked. "How much of your weight do they take?"

"Maybe a little," Raven called over her shoulder. "They're mostly for stability over rough terrain, though."

"I could probably use a pair," Kit said, and Raven told her there were plenty of outdoor shops in the trail towns along the way. Then, because everyone seemed so taken aback by her own spontaneous hiking philosophy, she asked, "How long did you plan your trip before you came here?"

"Almost exactly a year," Raven said, and now it was Kit's turn to go wide-eyed.

"I can't imagine doing *anything* for a year," she said. "I've worked ten jobs in the last five years, and gone through probably six different relationships."

"Serial dater?" Raven asked.

"Not intentionally," Kit said. "Everyone my age just seems to want to settle down, even if they don't say that's what they want at the beginning. I'm not ready for that."

"That's understandable," Raven said. "Who wants to be tied down in their twenties?"

"Try mid-thirties," Kit said, and when Raven just said, *Oh,* she laughed and added, "Let me guess – you thought I was Dodger's age, and now that you learn otherwise, you think I probably *should* settle down."

"I just met you less than a week ago," Raven pointed out. "I *did* think you were a little younger than that, but who am I to tell you to settle down?"

"What about you?" Kit asked. "You seem like the committed relationship type."

"Well," Raven said, pausing and making Kit wonder if she was uncomfortable with this subject. Then she went on, though, cautiously. "If I were in a relationship, I'd want it to be serious. But I haven't been with anyone in over three years. I think we're almost at the Dome."

The abrupt change in the conversation didn't escape Kit's notice. It was developing into a pattern the longer they talked. Kit was an open book, but whenever she asked Raven about herself, she offered up a little superficial tidbit, then changed the subject. Kit decided it was best not to push her, and focused instead on the changing trail ahead of them.

CLINGMAN'S DOME WAS A LARGE, spiraling concrete tower at the top of a long, paved incline. Standing at the bottom of the hill and looking up at the object of Raven's desire, Kit felt a little overwhelmed.

She was reasonably in shape and she used to hike in the parks with Sam on the weekends, but so far, the Appalachian Trail had presented a much bigger challenge than she'd expected. Kit didn't worry about it – the muscles in her legs would grow and she'd build up calluses where she needed them eventually. But hiking this morning with Raven made her realize just how far outside her element she really was.

Raven was a specimen to behold, her loose tank top showing off strong, athletic shoulders and hinting at womanly curves beneath – balanced, of course, by impressively toned calves and strong thighs that Kit's eyes lingered on as she walked behind her.

Kit, on the other hand, felt like a sweaty mess before they'd even begun the most strenuous part of the day's hike. It was all she could do to smile and pretend she wasn't red and out of breath every time Raven turned around to check on her. She adjusted her heavy pack on her back and looked up at the nearly forty-five-degree incline of the path that led up to the Dome, and wondered if she was about to make a fool of herself in front of a beautiful woman.

Her thighs were burning just looking at it.

"Do you think we can leave our packs at the bottom?" she asked. At the top of the Dome, there was a 360-degree view of the mountains, but once they'd gotten their fill of it, they'd be coming right back down the same way they came.

Raven looked around, then said a little hesitantly, "It

should be okay. We'll just leave them on the side of the trail where they won't get in anyone's way."

It was around ten-thirty in the morning and there were lots of other people making the trip up to the Dome. Most of them looked like tourists from the Smoky Mountain National Park that the Dome was located in, rather than thru-hikers like the two of them. Kit could tell that Raven was uneasy about the idea of leaving her pack unattended, and if she was alone, she'd probably carry it with her all the way to the top.

But Kit cared more about getting the thirty-pound monkey off her back than the possibility that some unscrupulous passer-by might try to steal her pack. She unbuckled herself from it and let it fall into the brush beside the path, saying, "If someone wants my stuff, they can have it. I'll buy *lighter* equipment next time."

Raven laughed, then reluctantly laid her pack beside Kit's, saying, "I saw a park ranger a little way back, so it's probably safe."

She took her canteen out of her pack and took a long drink, then passed it to Kit while she dug her phone out as well so she could take pictures from the top of the Dome. A few hikers passed them as they got ready, and then they started on their own trek up the hill.

"Do you think the view is really worth it?" Kit asked, and Raven laughed.

"Do you think you'd get as much out of the trail if you started skipping significant landmarks?" she shot back.

"I don't want to skip all of them," Kit objected. "Just

the ones where you have to climb such a steep hill just to come right back down again."

"It's not that bad," Raven said, although the fronts of Kit's thighs were already complaining. She'd found ways to torture quite a few muscles that she didn't even know she had since she started on this spontaneous journey. Raven took pity on her after a minute and said, "Keep your mind off the path and tell me what made you decide on a whim to get on the Appalachian Trail with very little prior hiking experience?"

"Are you criticizing me?" Kit asked, more curious than upset about it.

"No," Raven said. "I'm fascinated. Never in a million years could I just wake up one morning and decide to do something that I'd never done before. I have to work up to stuff."

Kit shrugged and said, "It was just good timing. A couple of weeks ago, I had a really bad day – like, *my boss fired me and my girlfriend dumped me on the same day* levels of bad."

She glanced over at Raven, blood rushing into her head as she watched for a reaction to her use of the word *girlfriend*. A small smile crept onto Raven's lips and Kit grinned, too. She was almost sure by now that she wasn't imagining the tension between them.

Her lungs were burning and they still weren't even halfway up the hill yet, so she focused on the conversation like Raven told her to and added, "The Appalachian Trail has always been on my bucket list, and when that happened, I realized there was no reason *not* to hike it. Escaping into the mountains is a much better way to get over a break-up than drowning in a tub of ice cream or having a series of one-night stands."

"Did you love her?" Raven asked, sympathy coming into her voice.

"No," Kit said. "I mean, yes, of course I loved her – I couldn't be with someone that I didn't love. But I was never *in* love with her. What about you? What's *your* aversion to relationships about?"

She was taking a gamble there since Raven clearly didn't like talking about herself, but Kit wasn't the type of person who would be happy if she spent the entire day talking about her own life. Sure, she could *do* it, but she was far too interested in what made Raven tick.

Surprisingly, she got an answer this time.

"I wouldn't say that I have an aversion. My last relationship was three years long and we were talking about getting married and buying a house together," she said. "But life has its ways of showing you when you're not with the person who's meant for you, and we just didn't make it. She couldn't be there for me at a time when I really needed her, and I don't really blame her. It was a difficult situation for everyone."

Kit raised one eyebrow, giving Raven a sarcastic look as she said, "That's so cryptic - thank you for sharing so openly with me."

Raven didn't offer any more details, a darkness falling across her expression, and when a family of four with young kids jogged past them on their way up the hill, Kit put her hand dramatically on her forehead and collapsed on a large rock at the side of the path.

"I can't go on," she said, taking a long drink from the canteen. "Go on without me – I'll only hold you back."

Raven laughed and her expression lightened – exactly what Kit was after – and then she held out her hand. "Come on, it's just a little farther."

Kit took her hand, letting Raven pull her off the rock, and emboldened by their discussion of past relationships, she didn't let go as they continued to walk. Raven squeezed her hand briefly and Kit started glowing from the inside out. She could have walked up a thousand Clingman's Domes in that moment, but she was relieved that there were only a few more yards to the top of the real one.

They released hands as they entered the circular concrete viewing area at the top of the Dome. The family that had passed them was enjoying the view – mom and dad standing together and looking out over the mountains while their two kids ran laps around the Dome. Kit and Raven had to leap out of their way, and then they went over to the railing.

The view really did go on for miles, a pine forest spread out in their immediate vicinity and mountains rising up in the distance. Kit exhaled wonder and said, "It's beautiful."

"Worth the hike, right?" Raven asked.

"Definitely," Kit agreed. She turned and looked at the profile of Raven's face. She was stunning in the late morning sun, and the fine sheen of sweat on her temples and shoulders only made her skin glow even more.

Eventually, the family made their way back down the hill and for a brief moment, Kit and Raven had the Dome to themselves. Kit put her hand on the railing next to Raven's, looping her pinky over Raven's and feeling something warm and tingly beginning to grow in her chest.

She wondered what Raven would do if she kissed her right now, the very idea bringing color to Kit's cheeks. Then Raven abruptly turned to her with a big smile and said, "I think I just figured out your trail name."

Kit smiled and said, "Please tell me it doesn't have to do with my poor showing on this hill."

"Of course not," Raven said. She was studying Kit's face, her eyes tracing over her mouth before coming back up to meet Kit's gaze. Then she said, "It's Parachute."

"Parachute?" Kit asked, confused.

"You're the type of girl who leaps first, then assembles your parachute on the way down," Raven said.

"That sounds like an insult," Kit said.

"No way," Raven answered. "You came out here with nothing but a desire for adventure, and trust that the mountain would provide everything you need. I think that's beautiful – even if it does scare me a little bit."

"Do I scare you?" Kit asked.

"Yes," Raven admitted. "But I like it."

"Well, I like my trail name, then," Kit said. "Parachute."

7

RAVEN

For the rest of the day, Raven could feel a heightened energy between herself and Kit. They kept stealing glances at each other along the trail, getting caught more often than not, and Raven longed to be inside Kit's head, feeling what she was feeling and hearing her thoughts.

She hadn't felt like this in a long time, and it seemed almost ridiculous to feel the budding excitement and potential of new love on the side of a mountain. She was here to battle her demons and leave them along the trail, but in all of her planning for this trip, she'd never imagined that she'd find someone like Kit to make those battles easier.

And she was so young – ten years Raven's junior in age, and even younger than that in attitude.

Raven decided that for once, she wouldn't try to think ahead. She would take a page from Kit's book and simply enjoy the moment, and the unexpected pleasure of falling for someone.

"So what's it like being a professor of microeconomics?" Kit asked as they hiked through the forest on the other side of the Dome. It wouldn't be long before they came to the next shelter, and they'd both started walking a little slower to extend the time that they were alone together.

"It's great," Raven said. "I teach a lot of freshmen who need the class for their general education credits, and most of them seem to think that I'm trying out some kind of advanced torture techniques on them. But then I've got some really engaged upperclassmen in my economic analysis class, and they're always good for an interesting debate."

"Why economics?" Kit asked.

"I spent a lot of time at the university when I was growing up, killing time in the library while my professor parents held their office hours. I always liked it and I wanted to follow in their footsteps," Raven said. "The liberal arts aren't really my thing though – in literature, there are so many different interpretations. You get to apply analysis in economics as well, but you have to back up everything you say with math and statistics. What about you? Why anthropology?"

"It sounded interesting," Kit said, "learning about what makes our collective humanity tick… besides, I heard all the hot girls studied anthro."

"Was it true?" Raven asked with a smirk.

"Oh yeah," Kit said, winking at her.

The trail bent to the right and then they were coming out of the forest to a clearing where they found their shelter for the night. They were alone after all and Raven was quite pleased with this turn of events. Kit went over to the lean-to, a smaller one that would probably sleep about ten at its maximum capacity. She sat down and drank from her canteen, and Raven dropped her pack and joined her.

"We're here kind of early," she said. "It probably won't be dark for a couple more hours."

"I told you we didn't need to start so early in the day," Kit said.

"If we'd left later, we would have hit Clingman's Dome when the sun was highest," Raven said. Then she held up her arm, pointing out her fair complexion, and said, "Do you think I would survive at the highest point on the trail with the sun baking down on me? I go through a bottle of sunscreen every two weeks as it is."

"Fair enough," Kit said, offering the canteen to Raven. "So what do we do here for the rest of the evening, then?"

There was something playful in her brilliant blue eyes and Raven was afraid to suggest anything in case they weren't on the same page after all. Eventually, she said, "I guess we get to relax for a while."

"That's a novelty for you," Kit said, teasing her. "Well, I know one thing I want to do."

"Oh yeah?" Raven asked. Suddenly, her breath felt trapped in the back of her throat as she waited for Kit's response.

"I want to cook a big meal," Kit said, and Raven exhaled. *Oh.* "My pack's way too heavy and I gotta get some of that weight off my back."

"Okay," Raven said, happy to have something to focus on besides the ever-increasing tension that she felt growing between them. She reached for her pack to dig out her camp stove and asked, "What do you have?"

"Lots of stuff," Kit said. She got out her food bag and started unloading it on the platform of the shelter, lining up a long row of granola bars, little bits of leftover candy, jerky, packets of ramen noodles, a jar of peanut butter, canned tuna, and bags of dried fruit and trail mix.

"No kidding," Raven said. "You've probably got two weeks' worth of food here."

"Beginner's mistake," Kit said. "So let's eat some of it and get it off my back. What looks good?"

"I bet if we mix a can of tuna into my alfredo pasta packet, it'll almost taste like tuna casserole," Raven said. "And I'd be lying if I said I didn't have my eye on that salt water taffy."

"It's yours," Kit said, picking up a couple pieces and putting them in Raven's palm.

Raven got out her sleeping pad and set it on the floor of the shelter for padding, and they sat side by side while she cooked the pasta and tuna over her stove. Kit got out her spork and they shared the meal out of the same bowl. After her first bite – and a nearly orgasmic *mmmm* that colored Raven's cheeks – she asked, "So what's your deal, Lone Wolf?"

"What do you mean?" Raven asked.

"You're unlike any other hiker I've encountered so far," Kit said. "Hell, you're unlike most people I know, on or off the trail. You're so reserved most of the time and you hardly ever want the conversation to turn to yourself, and yet I sometimes get glimpses of the real you that are just incredible."

Raven turned fully red in the face and she wasn't sure if she should feel vulnerable or attacked by this abrupt metaphorical undressing. She'd never had anyone reach so far inside her and pull out something even *she* wasn't aware of, and frankly, it was a bit unnerving.

"I get this sense that there's something powerful running beneath your surface – pretty deep beneath," Kit went on. "But you try so hard to hide it."

"I'm not trying to hide anything," Raven said meekly.

She was beginning to wonder if she *did* resent the imposition, but she had to admit that Kit was right about one thing. She'd gone out of her way to make sure her cancer battle didn't come up in the conversation, even though it was such a huge part of why she was on this trail. She didn't want Kit – of all people – to see her in that way, though. Not here.

Kit backed off. She took another bite of their makeshift tuna casserole and said with full cheeks, "I didn't mean anything by it. I just get the impression that you're out here on a mission to beat the mountains into submission or something, and I was curious about why. We can talk about something else. What's your favorite type of music?"

Raven poked her stainless steel spork into a couple of

noodles, thinking, and then before she could talk herself out of it, she said, "I had breast cancer."

Kit would figure it out sooner or later if they were going to keep hiking together and doing... well, whatever it was that they were doing. She kept her eyes down on the bowl of noodles, reluctant to read Kit's face. Raven had seen so many faces reacting to that news – her parents, her girlfriend at the time, her friends, even coworkers she wasn't particularly close with but who wouldn't rest until she gave them an excuse for why she had to miss so much work all of a sudden.

They were all the same. An overwhelming sympathy that sort of *melted* into their expressions and stayed that way every single time they looked at Raven after that. She might just have to pack up her equipment and leave right this second if she had to see that same look on Kit's gorgeous face.

"On the day my doctor told me I was cancer free, that I'd beaten it, I went straight home and started planning this trip," she said before Kit had a chance to start expressing her sympathy and replacing everything she knew about Raven with that big, flashing neon sign. *Breast cancer survivor*. "Then exactly one year after that, I set foot on the southern terminus of the trail. I'm here because I hated being seen as nothing more than my illness, of being pitied and fragile, and I'm reserved, as you put it, because I can't stand the thought of carrying that version of myself into the mountains."

Finally, she looked at Kit.

Her mouth was slightly agape and she was studying

Raven's face, taking all of this in. All the delicious sexual tension that had been building between them all day had vanished, as Raven suspected it would, but at least she didn't detect any traces of sympathy in Kit's expression – yet.

"I don't see a fragile woman," Kit said. "I see someone who's brave, fiercely independent, and who knows exactly what she wants and how to get it."

"That's because you never saw me laying weak in a hospital bed with bandages around my chest," Raven said. *In for a penny, in for a pound,* she thought as she unburdened herself to Kit. She was easy to talk to, and there were certain things that Raven could never talk to her own family about – they were too close to all of it. She said, "I lost my aunt to breast cancer when I was a teenager. She was about the same age I am now. That's something my mom has had a really hard time with, and sometimes even now when she looks at me, I can tell she's just waiting for the other shoe to drop – like she's waiting for a recurrence, or a complication of some sort to take me from her, too.

"It's hard for everyone in my family to walk around with a feeling like that, and I just couldn't take the weight of it anymore. I thought if I could come out here and conquer the AT, everyone would *have* to stop looking at me like I might fall apart any second. I know I'll never be the same person I was before I got diagnosed, but I'm done walking around with that cancer survival label over my head."

Kit reached over and ran her hand through Raven's

hair. It was messy, the pervasive greys that had increased in number since her radiation treatment obvious in the late evening sun. Raven closed her eyes for a moment at the pleasant sensation of Kit's fingers against her head, and then Kit said, "I don't see any labels. You're beautiful and strong."

8

KIT

Kit got brave and put her arm around Raven's shoulder in a slightly awkward, comforting hug. When Raven didn't object, she left it there and they let the heavy conversation drop. The shelter was situated on a small hill, just high enough to get a decent view of the sunset. The two of them were watching it together when three bobbing headlamps came up the trail toward them.

When they got closer to the shelter, Kit saw that it was Dodger, Break Time and Eagle Scout.

"Hey," she called to them. "You're cutting it a bit close to dark, aren't you?"

"We're not afraid of a little night hiking!" Dodger declared.

"What about bears?" Raven asked, shifting under Kit's arm and sliding a few inches away from her. Kit took her arm off Raven's shoulder and she started cleaning up the remains of their dinner from the shelter platform.

"Haven't run into any of those yet," Eagle Scout said. "Thank God."

The three guys came over and set their packs down on the shelter floor, then Dodger said, "You two have been hiking together a lot. I may have made a mistake in picking your trail name, Lone Wolf."

Raven smiled, then Kit said, beaming, "Oh, that reminds me – I got a trail name of my very own this afternoon. You can call me Parachute."

"Right on," Dodger said. "As in, jumping without one?"

"Basically," Raven said, laughing. "It suits her, right?"

"Yeah, it's a good one," Dodger agreed, and Kit pretended to be offended by this banter at her expense. Kit offered the guys some of the food she was trying to unload. Break Time took some of the candy, while Dodger and Eagle Scout helped themselves to a couple cans of tuna.

"I'm going to find the stream and wash out my cooking pot before it gets fully dark," Raven said, and Kit could tell that she was already starting to rebuild the walls that had come down so beautifully when she'd opened up about her cancer diagnosis. It was nice to see the real Raven for once, vulnerable and raw, but Kit understood why that version had disappeared again as soon as the guys showed up at camp.

While she was gone, the guys told Kit about the two days they spent hitchhiking from trail town to trail town, drinking ice cold beers and enjoying nights on real mattresses in the motels they found along the way. Then when Break Time and Eagle Scout started setting up their camp stoves to cook a proper dinner, Dodger took the opportunity to lean in close and look conspiratorially at Kit.

"Did I see you with your arm around Lone Wolf when we came up the trail?" he asked. "Or have I just been so out of touch with civilization that I'm seeing lesbian mirages?"

Kit rolled her eyes and shoved Dodger away.

He was a frat guy to the core, but he redeemed himself slightly as he leaned against the wall of the shelter and said, "I think it's nice. Now, if you catch me putting my arm around Break Time or Eagle Scout, please intervene because I've lost it."

Kit laughed, and then she saw Raven coming up the hill with her cleaned cooking pot in hand. She and Raven sat next to each other at the edge of the shelter, although Raven left a little space between them, and they watched the guys cook and eat their dinners while they daydreamed about how luxurious an old motel mattress could be, even if it *did* have springs that poked into your back all night.

"I've got a motel booked in Hot Springs," Raven said. "Granted, that's three more nights away, but it's nice to know there are a comfortable bed and a hot shower waiting every so often along the trail."

"I didn't even know people did that until I got out here," Kit said with a laugh – add that to the growing list of things she didn't know when she got on the trail. "I thought that once you were out here, you were just committed to the trail."

"I wouldn't survive," Break Time said. "I would literally have died in Georgia."

They all laughed and talked for a little while longer and then, when it was dark, Eagle Scout set up his tent by the light of one of the camp stoves and the rest of them laid out their sleeping bags in the shelter. Kit was surprised when Raven lay down next to her, but she didn't comment on it for fear that she'd change her mind.

It was nice falling asleep with Raven within arm's reach, even if there were two guys snoring lightly on the other side of her.

THE NEXT MORNING, Kit woke up to a surprising amount of sun streaming into the shelter. She looked to her right and found the spot where Raven had been sleeping was now empty, and she sat upright with the feeling of having slept through her alarm. It was late, and Raven liked to start early – did she leave Kit behind?

"Shit," she muttered.

"What's wrong?"

Kit looked in the direction of the voice and saw Dodger crouching in front of his camp stove, heating some coffee in his pot.

"Did you see Rav- err, Lone Wolf leave?" she asked. It wasn't like they'd actually *agreed* to hike together. It just sort of happened. But after last night, and all that chemistry yesterday on the Dome, Kit thought Raven would wake her when she was ready to go this morning.

She really didn't like the sensation that was growing in her chest, of how much she was starting to like Raven and the way it felt to be abandoned. *Hated it,* even.

"If by *leave* you mean *go take a dump*," Dodger said with a chuckle, "then yeah, she left."

"She's at the latrine?" Kit asked.

"Yeah," Dodger said. "She woke me up moving around so early in the morning and I saw her headed down that way a few minutes ago. Then I decided that if I have to be up at an unlawful hour such as this, I should have coffee. Want some?"

"Yeah," Kit said, feeling relieved and also somewhat twisted. The feeling of abandonment had only lasted a few seconds, but Kit absolutely detested it. For the last five years, she'd built her whole life around avoiding that feeling, so how had Raven managed to break down her barriers without Kit even noticing?

She crawled out of her sleeping bag and joined Dodger by the camp stove, and their conversation stirred Eagle Scout out of his tent. He poured strong black coffee for each of them and dug a few sugar packets out of his pack, and when Kit spotted Raven coming up the hill from the latrine, she had a sudden urge to run and throw her arms around Raven's neck.

That would be pretty silly, though, so she just sipped her coffee and when Raven joined them, she said, "Good morning."

"Morning," Raven said, a smile on her lips that was reserved just for Kit. "How did you sleep?"

"Not bad," Kit said, "but I can see why everyone keeps talking about mattresses. I'm starting to feel old beyond my years."

"If you want to come with me when I go into Hot Springs, I'm sure we can find a vacancy for you at the motel," Raven said, and Kit eagerly agreed.

Finally, after they'd all enjoyed their morning coffee and the morning sun was beginning to burn off the dew from the grass, Dodger went over to the shelter and kicked Break Time with his toe. Break Time rolled over on his back and threw his arm over his eyes, groaning and murmuring, "Five more minutes."

Then Dodger went into drill sergeant mode, shouting for everyone else's amusement. "Get up, maggot! Hup, one, two! Drop and give me a McDonalds Sausage McMuffin!"

Kit collapsed into a fit of laughter along with Raven and Eagle Scout, putting her forehead on Raven's shoulder as she swiped at the tears coming from the corners of her eyes. Break Time scrambled out of his sleeping bag, if for no reason other than to get away from Dodger's yelling, and then they all made breakfast, packed up their equipment, and headed back onto the trail.

Kit and Raven hiked with the guys for a few hours, then when the trail crossed a road that would take them into another trail town, they split off to yellow blaze some more.

"I hear it's supposed to storm pretty bad tonight," Eagle Scout said. "Are you sure you two don't want to come with us?"

"I want to hike every inch of this trail if I can," Raven said. "A little rain doesn't scare me."

"Me neither," Kit said, even though she liked the idea of sleeping with a real roof over her head instead of in a tent that was blowing in a cold wind. She'd decided the moment she saw Raven coming up the hill from the latrine this morning that she would go wherever Raven went, or as long as Raven allowed her to tag along.

So Raven and Kit said goodbye to the guys, and they had the rest of the day to themselves. They didn't pass any other hikers, and Kit enjoyed the time alone with Raven even though things had taken on a slightly different tone today.

Raven didn't look back to check on Kit as many times as she had yesterday, and Kit found it a little harder to come up with topics of conversation. As much as she wanted to forget about it, her mind just kept going back to how upset she was when she thought that Raven left without her. That was a feeling she desperately wanted to avoid.

They ended up talking about inconsequential things all day. Raven pointed out particularly pretty views and shared interesting bits of trivia about the trail, and Kit filled the silences with long-winded discussions of the television shows, books, and musical tastes that they had in common. Then in the early afternoon, the sky started to grow darker just like Eagle Scout had predicted.

"Here comes that storm," Raven said. "Right on schedule."

Kit turned her head up to the sky, where full, gray storm clouds were gathering and quickly blotting out the sun. She asked, "How far until the next shelter?"

"Five more miles," Raven said. "I'm pretty sure we're going to get wet."

"That's okay," Kit said. "Doesn't bother me."

It was less than twenty minutes later when she found herself eating those words. It was like the sky opened up and torrents of rain started sluicing down on them. Kit and Raven's clothes were soaked within seconds of the beginning of the downpour, and Kit laughed as rain plastered her hair to the sides of her face and made her clothes cling to her body.

Raven had to shout to be heard above the roar of the storm as she met Kit on the trail and said, "No way we're going to reach the shelter. Let's set up one of our tents and ride out the storm, then we can keep hiking if it lets up before dark!"

"Okay!" Kit shouted back to her. It was hard to even see the path in this much rain, but they eventually found a suitable piece of flat ground a few yards off the trail and worked together to set up Raven's tent. It was difficult, the wind and rain working against them, but they got the tent set up and staked and then crawled inside.

Kit pulled off her shirt, wringing it out as best she could outside the tent flap, and then did the same for her hair. She was laughing as she realized the futility of attempting to dry anything out in a downpour, and when she turned to look at Raven, her good mood met a wall.

"Are you okay?" she asked.

Raven was shivering from the rain, but she refused to take off her wet clothes. Instead, she was clutching her pack in front of her chest and doing her best to slick her hair back out of her face. "Yeah, fine."

Her answer was short and Kit could feel the distance between them like something palpable, even in the close space of the one-man tent.

"Do you want me to put my shirt back on?" Kit asked, looking self-consciously down at her sports bra. That was soaked, too, but there was nothing to be done about that. "I didn't mean to be forward – it's just that I'm soaked."

"It's not that," Raven said. "You *should* get out of your wet things, so they can dry and so you don't catch a cold."

"What about you?" Kit asked carefully. "If you'd rather be alone, I can go set up my own tent."

"I had a lumpectomy and they had to take a fair amount of tissue. I'm not really comfortable with the way my chest looks now," Raven said, refusing to meet Kit's eyes. "My shirt is clinging."

"Oh," Kit said. She didn't really know what the proper response was, but she wanted to say something comforting. She thought about *I promise not to look,* but that seemed pretty unlikely in a space this small, so she settled on, "I don't mind."

It wasn't the right thing to say and she knew it the moment the words came out of her mouth. Kit was no good in situations like this. She'd been running from anything serious in her life for so long, she had no experience with it.

Raven pressed her lips together and clutched her pack tighter, and Kit stammered, "I mean, it's not a big deal to me. I can't think of anything that could detract from your beauty."

Raven looked at her then, as a crack of lightning boomed overhead and the storm continued to rage outside. They were stuck in this tent together for better or worse, and it seemed like Kit's dumb mouth was determined to make it *for worse*.

"I'm sorry," she said at last, admitting defeat in her attempts to be comforting.

"It's okay," Raven said. "It's my problem, not yours."

Her teeth were already chattering slightly from the cold and Kit just wanted to reach over and pull Raven into her arms. Instead, she said, "Look, you can't stay in that wet shirt. I'll turn around and you take it off, then we'll just prop our packs up between us, like a makeshift privacy screen. Okay?"

Raven agreed and that's what they did. They sat awkwardly beside each other for a couple of minutes, trying to decide what to do next.

Kit listened to the storm and said, "It doesn't sound like we're going to get to the shelter tonight."

"No," Raven agreed. Then after another minute, she looked down at her lap and asked, "So, did it happen? Do you think of me differently now that you know?"

"No," Kit said, surprised. "Not at all."

"Then I was imagining things when I sensed that you were being distant today?" Raven asked. "It feels like something changed between yesterday and today."

Kit let out a long breath. The tent was beginning to feel humid from the heat of their bodies and the moisture of the rain on their skin. Raven had already been vulnerable with her and told her a secret that had been very hard to share. Kit had to do the same now, or else things really *would* change between them.

"You're not imagining it, but it's not because of you," Kit said. "Or, it's not because you had cancer. It's because I like you and I started worrying that you were going to live up to your Lone Wolf name and ditch me, so I subconsciously started pulling away first. It's kind of a thing that I do."

She tried to laugh to lighten the mood, but Raven just turned to look at her. There was honesty in her big brown eyes, and it made Kit want to open herself up – as painful and uncomfortable as that sounded.

"I told you I haven't had a great track record with jobs or relationships lately," she said, and Raven nodded. "When I first graduated college, I started seeing this girl – Monica. Well, it was a lot more than seeing each other. We ended up being together for five years. We were practically married and it was the most serious relationship I've ever had. One night, I got home before her, made us a steak dinner on the grill, and waited for her. And I kept waiting. The steaks got cold and rubbery and it was three more hours before her parents finally called to tell me she'd been killed by an impaired driver on her way home from work. On a Tuesday night at rush hour. How fucking unfair is that?"

"I'm so sorry," Raven said. She reached over their pack barricade and put her hand on Kit's shoulder. Kit put her hand on top of Raven's and a few tears slid down her cheeks, hot even in this warm tent.

Then she swiped them away and said, "It was the hardest thing I've ever gone through, and I decided that I never wanted to feel that way again. I stopped doing anything more than casually dating. Even when I did have a relationship here and there, I didn't really give my heart to anyone. I moved back in with my parents so that I could live without a lease holding me down. I stopped caring about my career because how can you even *think* about the future when a twenty-eight-year-old can get killed by a drunk driver on a road she's traveled every day for five years on her way home to her girlfriend?"

Raven reached over their packs and hugged Kit fiercely, squishing her backpack between them. Kit threw her arms around Raven and buried her face in the crook of her neck. She cried for a minute, letting all those deeply buried feelings rise to the surface for just a moment. Then she pushed them back down, cut off her tears, and sat upright.

"So there you have it," she said with an insincere laugh. "You feel broken on the outside, I feel broken on the inside. What a pair we make."

Raven wiped away Kit's tears, then said, "Thank you for telling me that. I feel like I have a better understanding of you now, as painful as it must have been to tell that story."

"I haven't told it to anyone in close to five years," Kit said. "The only people in my life who even know about Monica are my parents and a few other relatives. I left all my friends from back then behind because it was just too awful to keep talking about her all the time."

"Well, I'm glad you told me," Raven said.

Then she slowly dismantled the barricade between them, setting their packs at the foot of the tent. She was careful to turn her back to Kit as she did so, but then she took Kit's hand and lay down, pulling Kit's arm tentatively around her waist.

The rain outside had slowed to a steady patter on the sides of the tent, and Kit fell asleep with her heart pounding out the same cadence as the rain.

9

RAVEN

Raven tried hard to be mindful of Kit's emotional wounds without actually acknowledging them. That was what she wanted for herself – patience and understanding, without any overtones of sympathy or pity.

The next morning, they woke up to sunlight streaming into the tent. Kit's arm was still wrapped around Raven's waist and it felt so good, she hardly wanted to wake her. But nature was calling, and they'd lost ground when they had to stop early last night for the storm. So she carefully lifted Kit's arm and sat up.

Kit stirred, then woke.

"Good morning," she said softly, smiling up at Raven. She was glowing in the early morning sunlight, and Raven had a sudden and overwhelming urge to kiss her.

Instead, she just brushed Kit's hair out of her face for her and said, "Good morning. The storm finally let up.

You know, we're lucky that a bear didn't visit us in the night because we forgot to hang our food in the trees."

"Trail magic?" Kit asked, and Raven laughed, then handed her t-shirt back to her. Their clothes were a little bit crunchy and stiff from the rainwater, but they were dry and they'd be able to do laundry in two days when they reached Hot Springs. Raven was very much looking forward to it.

They spent the next couple of days hiking together with a newfound sense of ease with each other. It was something that Raven was pretty unfamiliar with, but it was nice to share a mile or two of silence without any need to fill it with meaningless chatter. She could feel Kit's presence behind or beside her on the trail, and that was enough.

That was wonderful, in fact.

They followed the white blazes out of the forest and walked across the wide-open plains along Max Patch Mountain, and spent leisurely evenings in the shelters, either alone or with other hikers. When they were alone, Raven had fun flirting with Kit and allowing a part of her to be awakened that had long laid dormant. She felt like a woman again and she felt very strongly drawn to Kit.

They didn't talk about Raven's cancer again, or Kit's girlfriend. Instead, they got to know each other and Raven had the very strange and delightful feeling of being on an endless date on top of a mountain.

Eventually, they reached the road that would take them into Hot Springs, where a shower, a comfortable bed, and Raven's next drop box was waiting. It was a two-lane road that intersected with the trail and led right into town, so instead of needing to hitch a ride to get there, all Raven and Kit had to do was follow the white blazes.

When the little town was visible on the horizon, Raven dug her phone out of the pouch on the outside of her pack and said, "I'm going to call my parents and sister, okay? I let them know when I reach every trail town."

"Okay," Kit said, walking happily alongside her.

"What about you?" Raven asked. "Did you make plans to check in with your folks?"

"I didn't even bring my phone with me," Kit said, and Raven couldn't help chastising her for that.

"What about emergencies?" she asked. "Kit, that's really dangerous."

"I know," Kit said, abashed. "When I left Asheville, my ex was still blowing up my phone so I just left it. I wasn't thinking."

"Well, I'm going to let you borrow mine after I'm done. You should call your parents and let them know how you're doing," Raven said. While they finished the hike into town, she called her parents, then Annabel, and smiled at Kit as she let them know that she'd found a hiking partner so they could stop worrying about her being all alone on the trail.

Then she passed the phone to Kit and tried not to eavesdrop as she called her parents and gave them an update on her adventure. When she handed the phone back to Raven, she thanked her, saying, "My mom was really glad to hear from me."

"I'm sure she was," Raven said as they crossed a concrete bridge over a river at the edge of town. "So what do your parents think about you doing this trip?"

"I think they've more or less given up on the idea of me being anything other than spontaneous and pigheaded," Kit said with a laugh. "They know I can handle myself, though. What about yours?"

"They're still worried," Raven said. "I can hear it in their voices when I call. But they understand why I'm out here."

ABOUT TWENTY MINUTES LATER, Raven was sitting on the edge of the bed in one of the ugliest motel rooms she'd ever been in. The walls were papered in faux brick and the bedspread was so busy it made her eyes hurt. Her resupply box was sitting on the dresser beside an old tube television, and two hiking backpacks leaned together on the floor.

When they'd gone to the motel office to check in, the manager said there were no more rooms available for Kit to get one of her own. That's how Raven had ended up sitting self-consciously on this king-sized bed, listening to Kit singing in the shower.

"I'm bad at love, oh, oh, but you can't blame me for trying..."

They'd already shared a tent, and neither one of them was unclear about the fact that they'd been flirting relentlessly with each other for the last few days, but the idea of sleeping beside Kit in an actual bed made Raven's heart want to climb into her throat.

She wasn't sure she was ready for it, but unless she was going to chicken out at the last minute and roll out her sleeping bag on the floor, it was imminent.

When the water turned off a couple minutes later, Raven barely noticed it over the pounding of her pulse in her ears. Kit came out of the bathroom with a towel wrapped around her chest. It only fell to her mid-thighs and slid even higher with each step into the room, and it made Raven swallow hard. She couldn't even remember the last time she'd been in a room with a woman showing her this much of her body, and she was having a hard time meeting Kit's gaze even though she showed no modesty at all about being in a towel in front of her.

"Your turn," she said, coming over to the end of the bed.

Raven jumped up before Kit could come any closer and tripped over her words as she said, "Thanks. I'll be quick."

She went into the bathroom and closed the door, taking a couple deep breaths as she turned on the water and stripped off her clothes. She knew they could get through this night without anything happening, but what really scared her was the realization that she *wanted* something to happen.

She folded her clothes and set them on top of the toilet, then stepped inside the shower. Dirt ran off her skin and circled the drain, and it felt nice to wash and condition her hair, even if it was only with cheap motel products. She and Kit would be able to wash their clothes this evening, either at the laundromat in town or in the bathroom sink, and that would feel nice, too.

When Raven went back into the room, having already put her clothes back on, she was relieved to see that Kit was dressed, too. She wandered into the room, feeling a little bit like a woman without a mission. She knew exactly what to do while she was on the AT – just keep walking forward and following the trail – but in this room, she was lost.

"So, what do you want to do?" she asked.

"Should we get dinner?" Kit asked.

"Yes," Raven said, relieved at such a practical answer. "Let's see what's within walking distance."

They left their packs in the motel and headed down the street, and Kit said, "It's kind of funny – the idea of *walking distance*. By the time you reach Katahdin, do you think there will be anyplace in the world that *isn't* within walking distance for you?"

Raven laughed and agreed with her, saying, "Maybe it's time to retire that phrase from my vocabulary."

A few cars drove past on the street, and they walked past a couple of fast food restaurants, then Kit pointed to a diner on the other side of the road. "What about that place?"

"Works for me," Raven said, and she was surprised

and pleased when Kit slid her hand momentarily into Raven's as they crossed the street to the diner. She smiled at her, then released her hand and held the door open for Raven.

"After you, my dear," she said, and Raven's heart climbed even further into her throat at the endearment.

10

KIT

The diner was surprisingly crowded for the size of the town, and a lot of the diners had that characteristic, long-distance hiker look – muscular and sun-beaten, wolfing down their food like it was in short supply.

Kit and Raven chose a table in the back of the restaurant, pushed up against a brick wall that was colorfully painted in a Barbie doll pink that made the diner feel playful and charming like so many of the other establishments that Kit had seen so far along the trail. They both looked over the menu, but it took them about five seconds to decide on big, juicy-looking hamburgers.

"The need for protein is real," Kit joked as she handed her menu to the waitress. "I've never craved it so much as I have this past couple of weeks."

"Yeah," Raven agreed. "We're not even at the halfway point yet and I'm already so sick of peanut butter and protein bars. I need *fresh* food. I think I'm going to order a salad, too."

"I don't know if I'll ever eat another protein bar when I get off the trail," Kit said with a laugh. One thing was for sure – she had a much greater appreciation for her food now that her days were spent marching endlessly under the hot sun. In addition to protein bars, she was ready to swear off fast food, junk food, and anything that came in a cellophane bag.

"When do you think that'll be?" Raven asked.

"Hmm?"

"When you get off the trail," Raven explained. "You said when we first met that you didn't have a particular distance in mind."

"Trying to get rid of me already?" Kit asked, putting her hand to her chest and pretending to be hurt as the waitress returned with a couple of sodas and straws. She set them down and Kit watched Raven tap her straw on the table to unsheathe it, then put it between her supple lips.

"What?" Raven asked as she caught Kit staring.

"Nothing," Kit said, a little smile forming on her lips. "I just felt an overwhelming surge of jealousy at that straw, that's all."

Raven laughed and a faint pinkness came into her cheeks – or maybe it was just the color of the wall reflecting on her fair skin.

Kit took a drink from her own cup, then said, "I'm not going anywhere. I'm having a lot of fun with you, and I'll probably follow you all the way to Katahdin if you'll let me."

Raven smiled broadly now, and there was something even more beautiful about her when she let her mask fall away and simply showed Kit her emotions. "You can follow me if you want to."

"Good," Kit said. "Because I intend to."

The waitress returned pretty quickly with their food, despite the number of other diners in the restaurant. She set down two big plates heaped with oversized burgers and French fries, as well as a large bowl of salad for Raven. The two of them dug in, and for a moment they were completely absorbed in their food.

When Kit finally looked up from her burger, Raven was staring at her, head cocked slightly to the side. Kit put the burger down, her cheeks still full of ground beef as she grabbed a napkin and asked, "Do I have sauce on my face?"

"No," Raven said. She narrowed her eyes, and asked, "Why do you like me?"

"What do you mean?" Kit asked, furrowing her brow.

"I just don't know what you see in me," Raven said. "I'm old and damaged. I've got gray hair, I hate the thought of anyone even looking at my body, and I've made it pretty hard for you to get to know me. I'm Lone Wolf, after all, and yet I can't seem to shake you."

She smiled as she said this last part, but the concern on her face was clear.

"Why do you keep trying so hard to know me?" she asked.

"I already do know you," Kit said. Beneath the table, where it wouldn't be conspicuous, she slid her boot between Raven's trail runners, nudging her foot. "And I don't see you that way at all."

"You will eventually," Raven said. "If we keep flirting with each other, it's inevitable you'll see that side of me."

"And eventually you'll see that I'm incapable of dealing with an event that happened half a decade ago," Kit said. "I'm immature and afraid to love anyone. You're afraid to let anyone get close to you because you're carrying around the crazy idea that you're broken just because of something tragic that happened to you. Sounds like a match made in heaven to me."

Raven laughed. "A dysfunctional match, maybe."

"Everything and everyone is dysfunctional," Kit said. "Anything else is a lie."

"You're probably right about that," Raven conceded.

Kit changed the subject and put on a superficial grin. "I don't know about you, but I think that's enough mutual self-pity for one meal. Tell me about the *best* day you've ever had."

She picked up her burger again and Raven thought for a minute, then smiled and told Kit about her after-college adventure, backpacking through Europe with her sister and the day they got to visit the little town where her grandparents were from and met their distant English relatives.

From there, they moved on to favorite vacation spots, hikes, and foods. And they flirted quite a bit more. By the time the check came, there was a rather serious game of footsie going on beneath the table, and Kit couldn't tear her eyes off Raven. She hated that Raven thought of herself as old, and if anything, the wisps of gray in her hair and the fine, barely noticeable wrinkles at the corners of her eyes enhanced her beauty.

At the very least, they gave Kit more to linger on.

When the waitress laid the check upside down on the table, Kit snatched it and paid for their meals, despite Raven's objections. Then they walked back to the motel, and Raven held Kit's hand in the dark.

As soon as they were alone and Raven slid the chain across the motel room door, Kit came up behind her and slid her arms around Raven's waist. She kissed her neck and Raven melted into her just as Kit hoped she would. She kissed her again, tasting her soft skin and inhaling the motel shampoo in her hair. It was such a generic scent, but even that smelled incredible because it was on Raven's body.

Kit had been craving this moment for so long. She kissed Raven's neck slowly, wanting to make it last for as long as possible.

After a minute or two, Raven twisted around in Kit's arms to face her, and finally, their lips met. She smelled like the afternoon sun and she tasted like sugar. Kit opened her mouth and kissed her harder, gliding her tongue along Raven's lips and then into her mouth. Raven let out a deep, ecstatic groan, but when Kit tried to hold her closer, she reached up and put her hands around Kit's neck, wedging her forearms between them.

"Are you uncomfortable?" Kit asked, pulling back

and resting her forehead against Raven's. She wanted her so badly, the space between them was painful.

Raven nodded, then said, "I'm sorry. I really want to kiss you, but I can't let you feel my chest."

She looked distressed. Kit took Raven's hands in hers, pulling them down from her neck and kissing her fingertips.

"Come on, let's take a breather," she said, leading Raven over to the bed. A breather was the absolute last thing she wanted right now, but she knew if she pushed Raven too hard, the Lone Wolf would reappear and push her away entirely. They sat down side by side on the edge of the bed with its scratchy, ugly comforter, and Kit asked, "Do you want to talk about it?"

"Not really, but we probably should," Raven said. "I like you, Kit, and I think you're really gorgeous and incredibly sexy. I *really* want to touch you, but I haven't been with anyone since my surgery. I really wish I wasn't so vain about how my chest looks, but I am."

"I don't think it's vain," Kit said. She ran her hand along Raven's cheek, then leaned over to kiss her. Then she said, "I think it's completely understandable and I just want you to be comfortable with me because I think you're so beautiful. Is there anything I can do?"

"I think I just need time to get used to the idea," Raven said. "Do you think maybe we could just go to bed? I'm really tired."

"Yeah, of course," Kit said. She kissed Raven again, then they took turns in the bathroom. They both put on motel robes and Raven washed their trail clothes in the sink and hung them from the shower curtain rod to dry, and then turned out the light and crawled into bed beside Kit.

She took Kit's hand and pulled it around her like she'd done that night in the tent when it was storming, careful to keep Kit's arm low around her waist. Then in the dark, she asked, "Are you disappointed?"

"That we didn't have sex? Of course not," Kit said, kissing Raven's shoulder and snuggling tighter against her back.

"I wasn't sure if you were picturing some kind of torrid trail love affair," Raven said. "I don't want to be a disappointment."

"You're not," Kit said firmly. "You're my favorite bit of trail magic so far. I'm really happy – and lucky – that I found you."

"So far?" Raven asked, pretending offense. "What does that mean?"

"Well, you never know when Dodger's gonna show up with an ice cold beer," Kit said. "That's pretty darn refreshing when you're sweating all your fluids out on top of a mountain."

Raven laughed and let herself relax against Kit, which felt just as nice as anything that might have gone on in their hotel room tonight.

11

RAVEN

Raven woke up the next morning with a warm body pressed against hers for the first time in more than three years. Before she even opened her eyes, she noticed the curves of Kit's breasts against her back and their hips locked together. Kit's breath was warm and comforting against Raven's neck and she lingered in the moment.

Kit stirred behind her, shifting her hips to snuggle against Raven, and desire bloomed warm between her thighs. She rocked her hips and pressed herself into Kit, undulating until she was rewarded with a soft, semiconscious moan against her neck.

Kit started moving her hips too, grinding against Raven and letting out little desirous groans as she became more aroused. Raven slid one hand backward and found Kit's hip, then inched down to her thigh. The very sensation of her curves against Raven's hand was enough to make her throb with need – she'd been aching for this moment for weeks. Kit parted her legs, allowing room for Raven to slide her hand further up the inside of her thigh as she kissed Raven's neck.

Then Kit slid her hand up Raven's stomach, and when her fingertips grazed Raven's ribs, she jumped out of the bed, her heart racing.

Kit sat up, looking alarmed, and asked, "What's wrong?"

"I told you I can't," Raven said, wrapping her arms defensively across her chest.

"Shit," Kit said. "I'm sorry. I was only half awake, and it was instinct."

"It's okay," Raven relented, feeling her pulse rate slowing back down by degrees.

"I was having fun, though. Were you?" Kit asked.

"Yeah," Raven said. "It felt really good."

"Come back to bed, then," Kit said. "I promise I'll keep my hands to myself."

"Mmm," Raven groaned, looking toward the window. The heavy curtains were drawn but she could see quite a bit of light trying to seep in around the edges. "I want to, but it must be getting late. We should get back on the trail."

Now it was Kit's turn to moan. "Please no. It's so much nicer being here with you. Can't we just stay a little while?"

"I can't," Raven said.

"Why not?" Kit asked with a frown. "Because of your itinerary?"

"Partly," Raven said. She pulled the curtains open to let the light in and erase any possibility of going back to bed. "And partly because I don't think I can stay in this motel room with you without making love to you. I'm not ready, and I don't want our first time to be something that ends with me crying and locking myself in the bathroom."

Kit reached out her hand and Raven took it, sitting down on the edge of the bed. Kit said, "I don't want that, either. We'll wait until you're ready. But does that really mean we have to hike today?"

She winked at Raven after this last bit and Raven laughed, then swatted Kit's behind through the sheets. "Yes. But I noticed last night that the diner has a pretty big breakfast menu. I'll treat you to some blueberry pancakes before we get back on the trail, how does that sound?"

"Sounds delicious," Kit said, sprawling lazily on the bed while Raven went into the bathroom to retrieve their clothes and get ready for the day.

THAT DAY WAS one of the best that Raven had spent on the trail. She had a full belly and lots of energy, and Kit kept her entertained every step of the way. All the uncomfortable tension between them was gone now and instead, they spent the whole day flirting and teasing each other.

Raven habitually led the way since she had most of

the journey memorized, but Kit would jog up to her every so often and grab her hand, spinning her around and surprising her with a kiss. Or else they'd pause for a quick hydration break and end up doing more kissing than drinking. They got caught at this once or twice by other hikers coming around a blind spot on the trail. Raven always pulled away bashfully, blushing and reaching for her canteen, but Kit just smiled and said hello to the interlopers, waiting for them to leave so she could kiss Raven again.

"I don't know about you, but I feel like a teenager getting walked in on by her parents," Raven said after the second time they'd been caught mid-kiss.

"Did that happen to you a lot?" Kit asked, raising an eyebrow at her.

"God, no," Raven said. "I didn't even come out until college, and I never would have invited a boy to my room."

"Well, then, it sounds like you're making up for lost time," Kit said, giving her another quick peck before Raven insisted that they get back on the trail.

She wasn't wrong, either. It was very liberating to feel so light and free, to give in to all the desires and impulses that had seemed like such distant memories over the last few years when more practical matters demanded all her attention. Raven's chest swelled every time she looked at Kit, and her core melted every time she had a chance to fall into those big, blue eyes.

After a while, she started to wonder if this was what falling in love felt like.

They reached the Roan Highlands about an hour before dark. They were a very long, flat stretch of elevated meadow higher than a lot of the surrounding ridgelines, and it felt a little bit like being back in Illinois, on road trips where farmland and flat highways stretched for miles in every direction. Except there were no highways here, and the mountains still surrounded them.

"It's like somebody dropped a field on top of a mountain range," Kit said, awed as they surveyed the horizon.

"Yeah, it's really beautiful," Raven agreed. She dug out her phone to take a few pictures of the view, taking the opportunity to snap a few candid shots of Kit as well, and then she started posing as soon as she realized the camera was pointed at her. Then they started walking across the wide-open field and Raven said, "We're running a little behind schedule today. We might have to do a little night hiking to get to our shelter."

"Or we could just camp here tonight, under the stars," Kit said.

"It's not a designated camping site," Raven reminded her. In the interest of leaving the wilderness as untouched as possible, hikers were discouraged from camping outside of shelters and designated areas unless there was an emergency, like the storm they'd encountered last week.

"We've been carrying our shelter on our backs for weeks. The *world* is our camping site," Kit said. "Come on – we'll be very respectful of the Highlands, I promise."

"It *would* be fun to watch the sunset here," Raven

admitted. "Let's just see how far we get, and if it's dark and we still have a long way to go, we'll camp here."

"Excellent," Kit said, smiling like a woman who had already gotten her way.

In the end, they stopped when the sky began to go pink and found a good spot to set up Raven's tent a few yards away from the trail.

Raven checked to make sure the ground was clear of rocks and other things that would be painful to sleep on, and Kit quipped, "If I'd known I was going to meet you, I wouldn't have even bothered with a tent of my own. It would lighten my pack a whole lot."

"Maybe there's a little more caution than I thought inside you, Parachute," Raven said with a wink. "Come here and help me set up the camp stoves for dinner before it gets too dark."

Kit obliged, and they both sat on Raven's sleeping pad while they cooked their dinner and watched the sky shift through brilliant shades of orange and pink and purple. By the time the sun dipped below the horizon, they'd finished their meals and were sitting with their arms wrapped around each other.

Raven kissed Kit on the head and said, "You were right. That was a beautiful sunset and I'm glad I got to see it from here."

"It pays to go off-schedule every once in a while," Kit said. "Well, is there anything else to do in the dark here, or should we go to bed?"

"I can think of one thing," Raven said, kissing Kit.

"Come on, let's get all this food cleaned up as best we can before bed so the animals don't sniff it out."

"Do you think a bear would come all the way out to the middle of the plains?" Kit asked. "There are no trees to hang our food from."

"Maybe that's one of the reasons why this isn't a designated campsite," Raven suggested. "Well, it's a bit late to camp elsewhere now. We'll just have to take our chances."

They put away all their food and put their packs inside the tent, then spread Raven's sleeping mat on the ground of the tent. The two of them stood outside of it for a moment after that, looking at each other in the dark and listening to each other's breathing. Raven's heart was beating hard in her chest, and after a moment of clumsy reaching, she took Kit's hand.

"We don't have to do anything if you're not ready," Kit reminded her.

"I know," Raven said. "It's dark, so that helps. Nothing above the belt and I'll be okay."

"Should we have a safe word?" Kit asked.

Raven laughed and said, "Just get in the tent, already."

"I think that's kind of long for a safe word, but okay," Kit said. She crawled into the tent and Raven followed her, zipping it closed behind them.

The space felt smaller than ever, with almost no moonlight at all penetrating the tent walls. Raven crawled forward until she found Kit's thigh, and then her lips as Kit leaned forward to kiss her. Raven let out a long breath and relaxed. She'd spent a lot of time worrying about this moment, and as soon as her lips connected with Kit's, she knew it was right.

She opened her mouth and let Kit's tongue in, while she slid her hand up from Kit's thigh to the edge of her shorts. Kit whimpered as her fingers traced the outline of her hip bone, then continued farther up. She lay down and Raven straddled her hips, kissing her and being careful to maintain a little space between their chests.

She inched her hand up over Kit's ribs and a shiver of desire ran through her as she found the curve of her breasts. She murmured in the dark, "Is it okay if I touch you? Or should we be fair about it?"

"Please touch me," Kit said, taking both of Raven's hands and putting them on her breasts.

Raven closed her eyes and let out a ragged exhale. They felt so perfect, soft and warm beneath her hands. She could feel Kit's nipples growing hard in her palms and she suddenly hated the little bit of fabric between them. She pulled Kit's shirt and sports bra over her head and put her hands on her again, and Kit moaned beneath her.

"That feels good," she said, wrapping her own hands around Raven's waist and rocking her hips against her.

Raven bent down and kissed Kit's chest, finding her breastbone first and then making her way slowly out to her breasts. She ran her tongue over one nipple, small and hard, and Kit bucked her hips beneath her, squirming with desire. Her own breathing was jagged now, too, and Raven wanted nothing more than to give her pleasure.

She turned her attention to Kit's other breast, licking and nibbling at the tender flesh while Kit filled the tent with the sounds of her desire.

"Oh, Raven," she said, squeezing her hips, "I like you so much. You're so beautiful."

"So are you," Raven said, kissing Kit's neck and then her lips. "I want you so bad."

"So take me," Kit said. She circled Raven in her arms and for the first time, Raven let herself rest fully against Kit's body. It didn't seem so bad in the dark. In this moment, she felt protected and loved. She felt safe.

Kit shimmied out of her shorts and Raven took off her pants but left her shirt on. They lay down beside each other again and Kit pulled Raven to her, wrapping Raven's leg over her hip and pressing her body against her. They moved together, kissing and caressing each other as their hips swayed in rhythm and their desire built.

Then Raven slid her hand between Kit's thighs, sliding her fingers into her wetness and eliciting an immediate cry of pleasure that tingled down Raven's spine. She ran her fingers up and down as Kit moved her hips to meet her, and when she found the hard nub of her clit, Kit's entire body clenched and held tighter to Raven.

"Right there," she breathed into Raven's ear, and Raven drew tight little circles with her finger as she felt Kit's thighs closing around her hand. Finally, when she thought Kit couldn't possibly cling any more tightly to her, she cried out in the most beautiful, fiercely arousing orgasm Raven had ever heard and collapsed against the sleeping pad.

Raven gave her a moment to catch her breath, then she asked, "Was it good?"

"Yes," Kit said, her voice shaky. "I'd walk *two* Appalachian Trails for another one of those."

Raven laughed, and then she felt Kit coming closer to her in the dark. She put her hand on Raven's neck to find her, then kissed her and laid her down on her back. She kissed Raven's cheek, then her jaw, and just when her heart was beginning to beat faster, Kit returned her mouth to Raven's and her hand skipped down to the hem of her shirt.

"Are you ready?" she asked.

"Yes," Raven said, surprised that she'd found her voice when she felt as small as this.

"What's the safe word?" Kit asked.

"Just get in the tent already," Raven said, laughing and feeling her body relax with the release. Kit knew just what to do to put her at ease, and she was grateful for that. She wasn't sure she could handle a moment like this with anyone else.

"Don't mind if I do," Kit said, kissing her.

Raven closed her eyes and focused on the sensation of Kit's fingers tracing over her body. She touched Raven's hip, and then ran her palm down the outside of her leg and back up her thigh. Raven parted her legs and felt the tip of Kit's finger gliding over her, softly at first and then applying more pressure as she swiped back down through her wetness.

It felt better than Raven had imagined – better than she remembered. It was like every ounce of her consciousness was between her legs, exploring right along with Kit's finger and delighting in the sensations that it produced.

She rubbed Raven's clit until it became slippery from her wetness and the sensation built, Raven's consciousness narrowing down until it was no bigger than the tip of that incredible, euphoria-inducing little nub. She felt herself getting hotter and wetter, tilting her hips to seek more of Kit, and Kit answered her. She slid her palm between her thighs and one finger slipped into Raven, sending a whole new set of sensations chasing each other through her body.

She moaned, the sound of her own pleasure surprising her, and arched her back as Kit moved her finger in and out of her slowly, bringing Raven closer to the edge with each stroke. When she added her other hand, rubbing small circles over Raven's clit while her finger continued its rhythmic pulse, in and out, Raven had to put her hands over her face. Her cheeks were hot and she felt something urgent within her, begging to be let go.

It only took another minute or two of Kit's slow, methodical touches before Raven was coming against her hand, her whole body contracting and her consciousness expanding simultaneously. No longer was she the size of a pinhead. Now, she could see the whole mountain from where she floated above herself. The orgasm shook her body for several minutes – longer than she knew an orgasm could go on – and when it finally subsided, Kit lay down again beside her and Raven threw her arms around her, a few happy tears cascading down her cheek in the darkness.

12

KIT

Kit and Raven were forced to contain themselves in the shelters for the next couple of nights. The Roan Highlands had been wonderful in their solitude, but the next couple of shelters that Kit and Raven camped at were packed with fellow thru-hikers. So they slept side by side under the stars in sleeping bags beneath the shelters, and they waited for their opportunity to be alone again.

During the days, they hiked and flirted and stole kisses as often as possible without sacrificing Raven's precious itinerary. Then on one particularly sweltering afternoon, Kit discovered a little bit of trail magic that lit her up with possibilities.

Raven was hiking ahead on a narrow part of the trail, and sweat had been pouring down Kit's back for the better part of an hour, making her shirt stick uncomfortably against her pack and flattening her hair to her head. Her shoulders were hot to the touch and even though she'd slathered on sunscreen from Raven's pack, they both seemed doomed to sunburn if they kept hiking through the hottest part of the day.

"We should take a break," Kit called up to Raven. "I'm almost to the bottom of my canteen and it's too hot for hiking."

"We will," Raven promised. "As soon as we find a good, shady spot."

She kept hiking, but Kit paused as something glittered in her peripheral vision. There was an even smaller footpath branching off from the trail, clearly not highly trafficked, and Kit shouted ahead, "Hey, wait up. I'm going to check this out."

Raven turned around and asked, "What is it?"

"There's a path," Kit said. She stepped off the trail and pushed her way through a few feet of overgrown brush, and sure enough, the thing that had caught her eye was a small lake tucked just a few yards off the trail. She yelled over her shoulder, "Raven, you gotta see this!"

Kit went down to the shore, where overgrown weeds made way for a small sandbar, and dropped her pack. The sun was even hotter out here, reflecting off the water, but it would feel a lot better as soon as she ran into it.

"Wow, it's so serene," Raven said as she met Kit on the sand and looked out across the water. The lake was only about a hundred yards around, hemmed in on all sides by more forest, and it felt secluded.

"It's our own private beach," Kit said. She took Raven's hand and said, "Swim with me."

"How deep do you think it is?" Raven asked.

"I don't know," Kit said. "Can you swim?"

"Yes," Raven said. "But it seems dangerous."

"Dangerous?" Kit scoffed. "It's a beautiful blue lake in the middle of our hottest day on the trail thus far. It's perfect."

She kicked off her hiking boots and pulled her shirt over her head, tossing it onto a large, flat boulder by the edge of the water. She fished the sandals that she wore around camp at night out of her pack, changing into them so that she wouldn't step on any sharp rocks beneath the water's surface.

Then she gave Raven a challenging look and pulled off her sports bra.

"What are you doing?" Raven asked, looking back at the little path that led them here.

"Skinny dipping," Kit said. "We can't walk around in wet clothes for the rest of the day."

"It might feel nice in the heat," Raven pointed out.

"Yeah, and it'll also lead to chafing and all-around discomfort," Kit countered. "Besides, it's way more fun this way. Come on."

Raven blushed on her behalf while Kit stepped out of her shorts and underwear and tossed it all on the rock.

"What if someone sees us?" Raven asked.

"We haven't passed a single hiker since we left camp this morning," Kit said as she walked into the water. It was just cool enough to be refreshing and she waded in deeper, then turned around when she'd gotten wet up to her knees and said, "If someone comes along, we'll just stay in the water until they move on. No one has to see our shameful nakedness."

Raven laughed, and finally she took off her pack. That was a step in the right direction.

"The water feels incredible," Kit said, walking carefully backward through the still lake until she felt it just beneath her ass. Raven was watching her intently, and from about twenty feet from the shore, Kit couldn't tell if she was looking longingly at the water, or simply staring at Kit's bare chest. She grinned and motioned to Raven with a come-hither look, then turned around and dove shallowly beneath the surface.

It felt good to be submerged, and the heat of the day immediately became more manageable as Kit came back up. She found Raven still on the shore and said, "Join me. It feels wonderful, and the sun looks so hot where you're standing."

She ran her hands through her hair to slick it back, then stood up again, the water coming to her waist and streaming in rivulets down her bare chest. Raven licked her lips – that much was unmistakable.

"You make it look so irresistible," Raven said, bending to search through her pack for her own pair of camp shoes. She took off her sneakers and changed into the sandals, then came down to the edge of the sandbar and stepped into the water, fully clothed.

"Boo!" Kit called playfully. "I don't want to be the only one skinny dipping!"

"I don't want to be seen!" Raven called back, and Kit knew that the possibility of being caught was not the only reason. Kit wasn't going to back down this time, though. Raven deserved a moment to enjoy herself, completely free of self-awareness.

"You have no idea how good this feels and I'm not letting you leave this lake without experiencing everything the mountain has to offer," Kit said. "I'm going to turn my back, and you're going to take off all your clothes and jump into this lake. Just tell me when it's safe to turn around again."

She turned toward the opposite shore, sinking down into the water until it was up to her neck so that the sun on the surface of the lake couldn't cook her any faster than it had been doing on the trail. Then she waited.

Faintly, she could hear the sounds of clothes coming off and water splashing as Raven eased her way into the lake.

"You're right," she admitted after a minute, and it sounded like she was a few yards away. "It does feel good."

"Parachute is good for a spontaneous idea now and then," Kit said, smiling even though Raven couldn't see it. The water started to move around her and Kit could feel Raven getting closer to her. The anticipation was almost as great as it had been when she was reaching for her in that pitch-black tent on the Highlands.

The next time she spoke, Raven was right behind Kit. "Okay, you can turn around now."

Kit turned around and found Raven crouching beside her, the water up to her collarbones. Kit moved a little closer and kissed her, keeping a respectable distance between them. Then she said, "Thank you for coming out here with me."

"Thanks for making me," Raven said, then she grinned and surprised Kit, splashing her from beneath the water's surface.

13

RAVEN

They played in the water for a couple of minutes, Raven taking care to stay crouched low in the water. It was a totally foreign sensation to her, being naked but for the cover of water, but she had to admit that it felt fantastic on her hot skin, and even a little bit freeing.

"So," she asked as she found Kit's hand beneath the water and pulled her closer. "Do you skinny dip often?"

"Not since I was a kid," Kit said. "You?"

"Every chance I get," Raven said, rolling her eyes. "I'm glad you saw this lake. I would have walked right past it."

"It can be good to look up from your section maps now and then," Kit teased, splashing her again. Raven turned her head, avoiding the brunt of the water, then brushed her hair out of her face.

After a while, they stopped splashing and just enjoyed the serenity of the lake. Kit floated on her back, her hand linked with Raven's to keep her from floating away, and Raven crouched in the water beside her. She looked toward the shore. They'd been enjoying themselves in the lake for at least fifteen minutes now and there hadn't been so much as a rustle of branches or a far-off voice to indicate that there was anyone else on this section of the trail. They really were alone out here, and Kit looked so free as she floated, her bare body presented to the sky without shame or embarrassment.

Raven let go of Kit's hand, crossing her arms over her chest, and Kit stood upright, asking, "Something wrong?"

"No," Raven said. She stood up so that the water came to her waist, her hands still protectively concealing her breasts, and said, "I want to show you. I think I'm ready if you are."

"Of course," Kit said. She smiled and added, "I'm glad you're feeling more comfortable with me."

"They're not even," Raven warned her, and the longer she went on, the more she started running at the mouth. She was nervous. "There's an incision scar about an inch and a half long over the top of my right breast, and the doctor had to remove some of the fatty tissue along with the tumor so it's not-"

"Raven," Kit interrupted. "I understand, and I'm not worried. You don't have to prep me because I think you're beautiful no matter what."

Raven nodded, hoping like hell that Kit was telling the truth. She was only in her thirties, and she'd probably never seen a scarred breast like Raven's. How could Kit know how she would feel when she saw her, any more than Raven could know how it would feel to let someone without 'Doctor' in front of their name see her breast?

She was committed now, though, and it was better to do it now than to continue wondering and worrying about this moment. She sighed, then let her hands fall away. Her shoulders were already heating up from the sun, but now her whole body felt like it was on fire as Kit's eyes went to her chest.

She studied her, really seeing her.

At least she didn't immediately look away. That must be a good sign, right?

Raven didn't need to look down to know what Kit was seeing. She'd seen it every day in the mirror, and it took her a very long time to be comfortable with what she saw. Compared to what some women went through – mastectomies and tissue loss, or even muscle loss and impairment of motion – Raven knew that her small scar and the asymmetric concavity at the top of her right breast was not so much to overcome. But it was *her* body, *her* expression of both her sexuality and her womanhood that had been irrevocably changed, and it had been a hard thing to come to terms with.

She wondered how Kit was doing with it.

"Well?" she asked, not sure if she was ready for the answer.

"I think you're just as beautiful now as I did five minutes ago," Kit said. "Your breasts included."

She stood up and came closer to Raven, and Raven looked away. "You don't have to say that if you don't think it's true. I know it's not much to look at."

"I would never say something that's not true," Kit said. She put one finger beneath Raven's chin and tilted her head to look at her. Then she added, "I honestly don't think it would be fair to the rest of the world if you were as incredible as you are *and* you had the most perfect tits on earth."

Raven laughed, then Kit splashed her lightly to break up the tension.

"You've got nothing to worry about and I see the same smart, fascinating, drop-dead sexy woman now that I saw the first time I met you," Kit said. She kissed Raven, then turned abruptly and called over her shoulder, "Catch me if you can!"

Then she dove into the water, splashing away while Raven jumped after her.

When they finished swimming, they climbed back onto the beach and put their clothes back on over their wet bodies. Raven found that she wasn't so quick to cover herself anymore, taking her time and feeling much more at ease with her body in front of Kit. Sure, they still had some ground to cover, but there were almost fifteen-hundred miles stretching out ahead of them and all the time in the world to do that.

Raven's tank top clung to her damp skin, and for the first time, she didn't mind. The irregular shape of her breast was visible, but it didn't bother her. It just felt good to have the lake water cooling her while they continued on their hike.

When they stopped for their next rehydration break, sitting together on a downed tree, Raven took out her section map and looked at the intersecting roads that were coming up along the trail. She turned to Kit and asked, "What do you say we improvise a little bit?"

Kit looked at her as if she was about to fall off the log. "Really?"

"Yeah," Raven said. She showed Kit the map and said, "Damascus is about a day's hike away. There's going to be a big festival there in two days and I had it all planned out to arrive just in time, but now I'm wondering if we shouldn't just yellow blaze into town now and enjoy an extra day of relaxation."

It would mean skipping about ten miles of the trail, and Raven had originally planned to hike as much of the AT as possible. But she was feeling good, she couldn't stop thinking how wonderful it was to meet Kit on the trail, and she could think of a thing or two that she'd rather do than hike ten miles that probably looked a heck of a lot like the ten miles before and after it.

"I'm not even going to ask you if some kind of alien slug creature found you in the lake and is now controlling your brain," Kit said with a huge grin. "Yes. Let's yellow blaze into town immediately."

Raven laughed and Kit jumped up, pulling her off the tree stump and along the trail. They hiked for another hour and found a road, where Kit immediately dropped her pack and stuck out her thumb for the next truck to come along.

THEY MADE their way into Damascus in the evening, just as the sky was going full dark. They went to the motel office and Raven explained that she'd made a reservation for the following night but she and Kit had arrived early.

"I'm not sure we can accommodate you," the clerk said, looking through the motel records on the computer that sat at the corner of the desk. "You know the Trail Days festival starts in two days, right?"

"Yeah," Raven said. "That's why we're here. We're thru-hikers."

"Well, if all else fails I'm sure you could find a trail angel in town who'll let you use their yard as a campsite tonight," the clerk said.

Raven glanced at Kit beside her, and she looked like she might not be able to take another night sleeping beside her and not being able to touch her – or worse, in separate tents entirely. Raven didn't like the sound of it, either. She asked the clerk, "Are you sure there's nothing you can do?"

He went back to his computer, and after a minute, he said, "Okay, you're in luck. I've got one room left, and it actually has twin beds for the two of you. That was lucky. You'll just have to check out of that room tomorrow at noon, then check into the one you originally booked with the queen bed. I'm sorry, but I don't think it'll be possible for you to keep the twin. Lots of hikers end up meeting friends on the trail to split costs with, and the double rooms are in high demand."

"We'll make do," Raven said as he passed a set of key cards across the counter to her.

"You're in room fifteen," he said. "Have a good night."

"You too," Raven said, handing one of the key cards to Kit.

They went down the sidewalk to room fifteen, practically chasing each other into the room. As soon as they were inside, they dropped their packs on the floor and came together in a passionate kiss. Raven allowed her body to press against Kit's, the first time since the Highlands, and the first time in a room bright enough to see each other's bodies.

They kicked off their shoes and drew the curtains, then Raven followed Kit over to one of the narrow beds. She took off Kit's shirt, then her sports bra. Kit allowed Raven to undress her completely until she was standing naked and vulnerable in front of her. Raven admired the subtle curves of her hips, and the youthfulness of her skin and breasts. She was perfect, untouched by time and ready to be completely open with Raven.

Suddenly, anxiousness snuck back into Raven, threatening to constrict her throat as she wondered if she was truly ready for this moment. It had been so freeing to let Kit see her on the lake, but what if this was too much for Kit? What if it was too much for *Raven?*

Kit seemed to hear her silent objection. She put her hands on Raven's arms, rubbing them comfortingly, and said, "You're in charge here. If you need to stop, just tell me."

"Thank you," Raven said. She took a deep breath and pulled her shirt over her head. She took off her pants and underwear next, and finally, her bra.

Kit put her arms around Raven and they kissed for a minute or two, Kit's lips and tongue reminding Raven of just how right it felt to be with her. Her courage returned, and she slid her hands up to Kit's breasts. As she did, she whispered, "You can touch me if you want."

She closed her eyes and felt Kit's hands on her, first the left breast, and then – tenderly – the right. Kit was careful and gentle with her, moving slowly and kissing her deeply. After a few minutes, they moved into the bathroom, barely releasing each other from their embrace, and showered the lake water off, and then finally, they pushed the two twin beds together and lay down.

14
—
KIT

Kit and Raven spent the following day lazily passing the time. They lingered in bed all morning, unable to keep their hands off each other, and Kit felt privileged every time Raven allowed her to touch her more intimately. She was still self-conscious of her body, but Kit could see signs that Raven was beginning to see herself through Kit's eyes – beautiful, strong, and no longer a damaged woman despite her scars.

And for her part, Kit felt something beginning to change inside of herself. She'd spent so long running from other people and the possibility of opening herself up to them, but it was different with Raven. Kit had nowhere to run, both when they were on the trail and now that they were holed up in this small motel room, so she started to open up by degrees and let Raven in.

She found that she *wanted* to do it, and that was the strangest feeling of all.

It was probably time – five years was long enough –

and Kit couldn't think of anyone else in the world she would want to be vulnerable with besides Raven. At least they could understand each other.

It was almost noon by the time they finally emerged from the motel room, in part because the motel clerk needed to prepare the room for its next set of inhabitants and in part because their stomachs were growling. So Kit and Raven gave up their room and shouldered their packs to explore Damascus for the day.

They found a diner and ordered a late breakfast, and while they were eating, another pair of hikers sat down at the table beside them. They were a man and woman both wearing plain gold bands on their ring fingers – probably husband and wife.

"Hey," the guy said, reaching across the space between their tables to shake Kit's hand, then Raven's. He looked like he was in his late thirties, with the start of a receding hairline, and his companion was about the same age, with sunbaked skin and a friendly smile. "We're Campfire and Marshmallow. Are you here for Trail Days?"

"Yeah," Kit said. "We got in a day early to relax a bit. I'm Parachute and this is Lone Wolf."

"Maybe if you're up for a little bit of manual labor, you can come work on setting up the music stage," Campfire said. "I heard the festival organizers give out free tickets to people who help with set-up."

Kit looked to Raven, and she nodded. "We might as well. We can't check into our motel room for the night until two."

Their food arrived – pancakes the size of dinner plates, with heaping sides of bacon and hash browns that Kit had no trouble wolfing down with the appetite she'd worked up. They spent the meal chatting with Campfire and Marshmallow – they were fellow thru-hikers who had come all the way from Portland to hike the trail on an extended honeymoon.

Then with their bellies full, the four of them made their way over to the large, open area of grass where the majority of the Trail Days activities would take place. From the looks of it, with stages, food trucks and vendor tents being erected all along the street, the festival would take over the entire town when it began.

Campfire and Marshmallow found work at the main stage, and Raven and Kit ended up helping about a dozen other festival volunteers as they set up a big white tent and dozens of folding chairs for a workshop area.

They lost track of their new friends after a little while, and when the heat of the day became too much, Kit grabbed Raven's hand and whispered in her ear, "I think it's time to check into that second motel room. What do you think?"

The next room was a little bit nicer than the first, with a spacious queen-sized bed that immediately drew Kit's attention. They showered together and then Kit pulled Raven onto the bed, and they stayed in it all night long, not even getting out for dinner. Kit found a brochure with a list of Damascus restaurants in it on the bedside table and they ordered a pizza, then sat on the bed as they ate it, the looks in both their eyes unmistakable.

I'm going to take you again the moment this pizza box is empty, if not sooner.

THE NEXT MORNING, Kit woke up to the hum of voices and activity outside. It was still early, but the great hiker migration to Damascus had begun. Raven was still sleeping soundly beside her, and Kit watched her sleep for a moment before she went to the window and parted the curtains to look outside.

The motel was on the main drag, so she had a pretty good vantage point to look at all the activity. She could see dozens of hikers on the sidewalks, and vendor tents going up all along the road to sell food, t-shirts, and small trinkets that were designed not to weigh hiker's packs down – magnets and keychains to commemorate their time on the trail.

It was barely nine a.m. and Kit could already smell the delicious aroma of fried funnel cakes wafting inside the motel room.

Farther down the street, she could just make out the music stage, where no one was performing just yet but dozens of hikers had already begun to lay out blankets and relax on the sunny field.

"Did it start already?" Raven asked from the bed, her voice a little froggy from sleep.

Kit crawled back in bed with her, wrapping her arms

around Raven and kissing her. "Not officially, but there are a lot of people out there. Do you want to check it out?"

"Yeah," Raven said, then she slid her hand over Kit's chest and added, "and also no."

"We can do both," Kit said, sighing beneath Raven's touch. "Come on, let's take a shower."

They made love in the shower, then got cleaned up and left everything except their money and Raven's phone in the motel room before heading out to explore the festival. Damascus had seemed like a small town yesterday, when it was just Kit, Raven, the locals, and some festival volunteers. Now, though, there were a few thousand hikers here, with more streaming in from the trail and surrounding towns every minute.

Kit dragged Raven over to the first funnel cake stand they came across, unable to resist the alluring smell of fried dough and powdered sugar. They found another vendor selling coffee and sat down at a picnic table near the music stage to eat breakfast. A festival volunteer came around and gave them a program, and Kit and Raven flipped through it together while they ate, making note of bands and workshops that they might be interested in.

"What should we do first?" Kit asked, her mouth full of delicious funnel cake.

"Let's take a lap around the festival and get the lay of the land," Raven suggested. It was so pragmatic – a very Raven thing to suggest – but Kit agreed it was a good idea.

"Maybe we'll see some people we know," she said.

"I'm sure Dodger, Break Time and Eagle Scout will want to experience Trail Days."

"Ooh, there's a guided hike for foraging edible mushrooms in the afternoon," Raven pointed out. "We should go to that."

Kit laughed, then asked, "You want to go on a hike? We've *been* hiking."

"I'm sure it's not a long one," Raven said. "I think it'll be fun."

"Okay," Kit said. "Let's do it."

She laughed again, and Raven looked at her with consternation. "You don't have to come along if you're just humoring me. You can stay here and watch the bands or something."

"It's not that," Kit said. She reached over and swiped Raven's chin with a napkin, then said, "I was having a hard time taking you seriously with the powdered sugar beard you were sporting."

Raven rolled her eyes, but she said, "Thanks."

"You're welcome," Kit said. "And I'd love to forage for mushrooms with you."

"Well if it isn't Lone Wolf and Parachute!"

Kit and Raven both turned as a familiar voice shouted their trail names above the noise of the crowd. Dodger was jogging toward them, with Break Time and Eagle Scout trailing behind him.

"Speak of the devil," Raven said. "We were just wondering if you yellow blazed all the way to Katahdin by now."

"Almost," Eagle Scout said, looking a little grumpy as

he caught up to Dodger and the three of them joined Kit and Raven at the picnic table. All three of them had clear plastic cups full of frothy beer in their hands, enjoying the festival to its fullest already.

"He's just angry because we're not getting as many miles on the trail as he wanted," Dodger explained, giving Eagle Scout a playful shove. "I told you not to expect a full-on thru-hike."

"Still way more hiking than *I* want," Break Time said, downing the rest of his beer. "I'd be happy to stay here for the rest of the trip and just hang out. Damascus seems cool."

"Yeah, it does," Raven said. "Kit and I got in two days ago and we helped set up the workshop tent yesterday. Everybody seems really nice here."

"Got here early, huh?" Dodger said. "Lone Wolf, the consummate over-achiever. So how have you two been?"

"Good," Kit said, looking sideways at Raven and trying not to give too much away. "We found this beautiful, warm lake a few days ago and went swimming, and before that, we camped on the Roan Highlands. The view of the stars was spectacular – I've never seen a sky so clear and unpolluted with light."

"Wow, you two have really coupled up," Dodger said. "I almost feel bad for naming you Lone Wolf. I'm not sure it suits you anymore."

Raven gave him a little half-smile, and Kit could tell that his comment wasn't sitting well with her but she wasn't sure why. Raven brushed it off, though, and said, "I guess that's the point of the trail – to challenge you. So have you guys been doing *any* hiking lately? Or are you just trail town hopping now?"

"Yeah, here and there," Dodger said. Then he turned to Break Time and laughed, saying, "Oh, man, tell them about the bears!"

"You guys saw bears?" Kit asked, her eyes going wide.

"Saw them? We were practically turned into bear food," Eagle Scout said. Dodger was still laughing and Eagle Scout said, "It's not funny, Brian. It was dangerous."

"It's funny because we got out unscathed," Dodger said. He nudged Break Time with his elbow and said, "Go on, tell them."

Break Time rolled his eyes, then did as he was told. He set down his empty beer cup and leaned across the table to tell the dramatic tale.

"Okay, so we're hiking this narrow part of the trail somewhere in the Smoky Mountains. I don't remember exactly what part, do you guys?" he asked, turning to his comrades. They both shook their heads, so he went on, turning his attention back to Raven and Kit. "We were on the side of a steep hill. Trees on our right, and a sharp drop-off on our left. Not a lot of places to go except forward or backward along the trail. We hear rustling in the trees to our right so we pause, and not ten seconds later, a black bear comes down off the hill and walks across the trail. It looks at us for a second, then continues down the drop-off. We think all's clear, so we keep going, watching the bear do its thing at the bottom of the valley there. Then, about thirty seconds later, we hear another rustling in the trees and see two bear cubs."

"I immediately say, 'Oh, shit! Go back,'" Dodger cut in. "Obviously, we got in between mama and her cubs, and she starts back up the hill toward us, *not* looking very happy. Meanwhile, this idiot *runs for it*."

"What would you have done?" Break Time asked Raven and Kit, looking resentful. "Dodger and Eagle Scout are just standing there like they can reason with the bear, and all I thought was *I gotta get out of here*. So I ran and when I finally felt like it was safe to look back, I noticed that they didn't follow me. They were still between mama bear and her cubs, and she was coming up the hill toward them. I watched the whole thing from the other side and I swear, Eagle Scout was on the verge of shitting himself."

"A perfectly justifiable response," Eagle Scout said, folding his arms across his chest.

"So mama bear comes back onto the trail and bares her teeth at us," Dodger picks up. "The message is clear – back the hell up. So we do, slowly walking backward along the trail. The whole time, I'm just praying we don't trip on a rock or a tree root or something and go flying down the hill ourselves. The bear marches us back until we're clear of her cubs, then she gives them the go-ahead signal and they come down from the trees and all three of them go down into the valley. That was when Eagle Scout and I had about three delayed heart attacks each and I tore into Break Time for leaving us there to die."

"Holy crap," Kit said. "That's incredible."

"It was pretty cool after the fact, when we realized that nobody was going to die," Break Time said, laughing.

"You guys should be wearing bear bells," Raven chastised. "I think there are vendors around here selling them."

"We have bear bells," Eagle Scout said. "Except *I'm* the only one who thinks they're worth wearing, even *after* all that."

"Who wants to sound like freakin' Santa Claus all day long?" Dodger asked. He finished his beer, then said, "Ah, anyway, it makes for a great story to tell when we get home. I'm going to get another beer. Anyone else?"

"Yeah," Break Time said, and Eagle Scout got up as well.

Kit and Raven weren't quite ready to start drinking so early in the day, so the guys went off in search of more alcohol and they stayed behind to finish their funnel cakes. Dodger told them that their plan for the festival was simply to get drunk and listen to music, and he said he'd save Kit and Raven a spot on the field in front of the stage to join them later.

They spent the first couple of hours of the day wandering through the festival, looking at all the different vendor tables and checking out a few different workshops, including the mushroom one that Raven was so interested in. Kit learned that chicken of the woods does *not* taste like chicken, as much as their guide tried to convince the group otherwise, and that she'd prefer to carry her food on her back, even if it did add a few extra pounds to her pack weight.

Then in the early afternoon, they went back to the stage area with a couple of cups of beer of their own and found the guys spread out on a tarp in the grass. Kit and Raven sat down with them and listened to a band playing reggae rock covers while they sipped their beers.

It was warm and there were thousands of people either sitting on the grass, enjoying the music or moving around the perimeter of the festival. Kit's beer was cold and her belly was full of fried food and wild mushrooms. Raven's lap looked inviting, and after her cup was empty, Kit lay down with her head on Raven's thighs, smiling up at her.

Raven played with Kit's hair, running her fingers through it in the most soothing way, and Kit closed her eyes after a while. The sun was pink through her eyelids. She turned her head toward Raven's stomach and fell asleep.

WHEN KIT WOKE UP, there was a different band on the stage and the music had turned into a Dave Matthews-esque jam session. Raven looked down at her when she stirred and Kit asked, "How long have I been out?"

"About an hour," Raven said. "I was just about to wake you because my legs were going numb."

"I'm sorry," Kit said, sitting up. Dodger and Eagle Scout were playing war with a deck of Trail Daysbranded cards, and Break Time was sleeping on the edge of the tarp.

"That's okay," Raven said. "I liked having you asleep in my lap."

"I'm kind of hungry again," Kit said. "Do you want to stretch your legs and find something to eat?"

"Sure," Raven said. They got up and bid farewell to the guys, then wandered out of the field and found a corndog stand along the street. It was getting late in the afternoon and a lot of people seemed to be following Dodger and his men's example, partaking heavily of the cold, refreshing beer available at stands all over the festival. Raven and Kit got another round for themselves after they finished eating, then wandered aimlessly through the festival for at least an hour.

They could hear the music wherever they went, carried on the wind, and it was a really peaceful way to spend an afternoon. After a while, Kit got brave and took Raven's hand, and they swung their entwined hands between them as they walked.

They ran into Campfire and Marshmallow briefly in the workshop tent, where volunteers were giving out foot massages. Raven asked Kit if she wanted one, but Kit leaned in and whispered, "I don't want to watch another woman touch your feet. If you want one, I'd be happy to help."

"I'm going to hold you to that," Raven said. "As soon as we get back to the motel room tonight."

"Deal," Kit said.

They kept wandering through the festival, and eventually they came to the edge of town. There was a little playground there, not a part of Trail Days but something that Damascus children must amuse themselves with on cool summer nights. Kit lit up immediately when she saw it and dragged Raven over to the swings.

"Come on," she said. "You can push me on the swing set in exchange for that foot massage."

She set her beer carefully on the ground and sat on one of the swings, kicking her feet to push off from the ground. Raven smiled as she watched her, then she put her beer down next to Kit's and went behind her to push.

On her next swing backward, Kit felt Raven's hands low on her hips, pushing her forward. Kit closed her eyes and felt the wind in her hair as she pumped her feet to go higher.

"This is turning out to be a really perfect day," she said as she felt Raven's hands on her again. "I'd be content to just stay here in this moment forever."

"I wouldn't," Raven said.

Kit put her feet down on her next backswing, twisting until the chains of the swing crossed and she was facing Raven. "You're not happy right now?"

"I am," Raven said, trying to reassure her with a kiss. "But I can't stay here. I haven't gotten what I need from the trail yet."

"I got more than I was expecting," Kit said, wrapping her legs around Raven's hips to hold the swing in place. Raven looked around, a little self-conscious, but they were alone on the playground.

"I did, too," Raven said. "But I'm not finished yet."

"Then neither am I," Kit said. "I told you before and I'll say it again, I'm going all the way to Katahdin with you if you'll have me."

"Of course," Raven said. She twisted Kit back around so that she was facing Damascus and the festival, then started pushing her again. She seemed a little bit off today, but then again, Kit herself was slightly buzzed from the unaccustomed alcohol in her system and the heat of the day wasn't helping. Raven probably felt the same.

"By the way," Kit said after a minute or two, "I really appreciate you letting me hike with you. I didn't expect it after I learned what your trail name was, but I really don't think I would have made it as far as I have without you, and I *know* I wouldn't have wanted to."

"I'm glad you're hiking with me," Raven said. "Being a lone wolf is overrated. And for what it's worth, I think you've come a long way since the day I met you, Parachute."

Kit dug her heels into the ground again, stopping the swing. She got up and went over to Raven, kissing her briefly. Then she said, "What do you say we get out of here? Trail Days is fun and all, but I can think of a few other things I'd like to do while we have the luxury of a motel room all to ourselves."

"I think that sounds wonderful," Raven said. They grabbed their beers off the ground and finished drinking them as they made their way back up the length of the festival.

When they got to the motel again, it was hopping

with partying hikers. They were all much drunker than Kit and Raven, hanging out on the lawn, talking and laughing with each other. A few of them invited Kit and Raven to party with them, but they politely declined and headed back to their room.

With the door closed, they could still hear the party going full-blast outside, but nothing in the world mattered to Kit except the woman in front of her. She slid the chain across the door and stepped out of her sandals, padding across the motel carpet to Raven.

"You are truly an incredible woman," she said as she put her hands around Raven's waist. "I want to spend the rest of my life in this motel room with you."

Raven laughed and said, "I think you're a little drunk."

"I think you are, too," Kit said.

She circled Raven in her arms and they fell onto the bed, their limbs entwined and their bodies seeking each other. They made love again, a little clumsily this time as they were unaccustomed to the alcohol in their veins after such a long time on the trail. But they were determined, and afterward, Kit spent a long time with her hands on Raven's feet, kneading out the knots and aches of the trail as she had promised to do.

"We should stay in more trail towns along the way," Kit said as she massaged Raven into a supremely relaxed state. "We could start our own Appalachian Trail blog, only instead of talking about all the awesome things you can see along the way, we'll only talk about the motels, rating them according to how nice the beds are."

Raven laughed, then she said, "That's a nice idea, but it would cost so much money to stay in town all the time, and it would seriously derail my schedule. Tomorrow, we've got to get back on the trail."

Kit groaned in an exaggerated way, then crawled up the bed and lay down next to Raven. She'd left her shirt off after they made love and for the first time, she hadn't bothered to cover up with a sheet or towel. Kit let her eyes linger over Raven's chest, tracing the slightly jagged appearance of the little pink scar on her breast.

The more comfortable Raven was with her, the more beautiful Kit found it.

15

RAVEN

Raven woke up the next morning with a pulsing headache and a little bit of nausea that increased when she sat up. It was quiet outside and she could tell that it was still very early, even with the curtains drawn across the window. All the revelers from last night must still be asleep, and for that, Raven was grateful.

She wasn't much of a drinker in general, and the beer yesterday had gone straight to her head.

She looked at Kit sleeping peacefully beside her, her leg thrown over Raven's thigh. How had they gotten so intimate, so fast? It had to be the trail and the strange bond that formed from spending twenty-four hours a day with a stranger on the side of a mountain. Kit didn't feel like a stranger anymore – not at all – and it sort of scared Raven to think about that.

Kit was so young. Ten years younger than Raven, and decades younger in terms of maturity and life experience. She couldn't possibly be feeling the same way that Raven felt right now, or maybe it was just the lingering effects of the alcohol making her feel anxious.

She slid out from under Kit's leg, careful not to wake her, and went into the bathroom to take a shower. She stood under the water for a long time, trying to wash her hangover down the drain. It was too hot, and the room was not air conditioned. She suddenly felt claustrophobic and the mountain was calling to her. She'd been away from the trail for too long and she really needed to get back to her journey.

The shower helped, and by the time Raven came back into the room with a towel wrapped around her, the nausea had subsided. Her headache, on the other hand, was still going strong.

"Morning, babe," Kit said from the bed. "You're up early."

"It's too hot to sleep late," Raven said. "I don't know about you, but I'm ready to get back on the trail."

"Sure," Kit said, although she didn't say it with much conviction. She sat up, letting the sheets fall down to her lap, and despite her headache, Raven had to acknowledge the strong urge to crawl back into bed with her at that sight.

"You don't have to if you'd rather stay here," Raven said. "There are still two more days of the festival. You could catch up with me later if you want."

Kit frowned. "Are you trying to get rid of me?"

"What?" Raven asked. "No."

"It kind of sounds like you are," Kit said. "Am I becoming a pest?"

"God, no," Raven said. "It's just that last night you were talking about yellow blazing. You brought it up more than once so I was wondering if you're getting sick of hiking. I know you never planned to hike this long."

"Plans change," Kit said. "And last night I was drunk. I want to keep hiking with you."

"Okay," Raven said. "Well, go take a shower and we'll get on the road in about an hour."

"Yes, ma'am," Kit said. She climbed naked out of the bed and came over to Raven, reaching for her towel. She tried to tug it away but Raven held it and Kit frowned. "Is everything okay?"

"Yeah," Raven said. "I've just got a little bit of a hangover. How are you feeling?"

"Peachy," Kit said.

"The perks of being young, I guess," Raven said wryly. "Enjoy it while you can."

"I'm not *that* much younger than you," Kit pointed out. Then she left Raven alone and went into the bathroom to shower. Raven found her canteen in her pack and finished off the little bit of warm water that had been left in it when they hiked into Damascus two days ago, then waited for Kit.

They made their way through town about forty-five minutes later. There were a few other hikers already out and about, but none that Raven and Kit recognized. Just on the edge of the festival, Raven paused and gave Kit another chance to stay behind and enjoy the festival. She said, "Are you sure you want to keep hiking with me? I don't want you to sacrifice your experience of the trail just because you're following mine so strictly."

Kit just shook her head.

"Babe, the moment I met you, my experience of the trail *became* you," she said. "So where are we hiking today?"

"The Grayson Highlands," Raven said.

They paused one last time in Damascus for Kit to get a funnel cake for the road, and because the thought of greasy food made Raven's stomach queasy all over again, she just got a handful of apples from another vendor and put them in her pack for later. It would be nice to have some fresh fruit when she was feeling better, which she was sure would not be long once she had a chance to burn off the alcohol in her system.

They walked down the street out of Damascus until Raven spied a familiar white blaze painted on one of the trees along the side of the road, and they stepped back onto the trail.

"Here we go again," Kit said, powdered sugar from her funnel cake falling down the front of her shirt.

She brushed it away and Raven laughed in amazement, asking, "You're really not the slightest bit sick today?"

"I drank two beers," Kit said incredulously. "I mean, they were pretty generously sized beers, but it's not like I got wasted. Now, Dodger and his buddies – *they're* probably having a pretty miserable morning."

Raven laughed again, but it made her head throb so instead, she just focused on the trail ahead of her.

Kit noticed and asked, "You sure you're feeling okay?"

"Yeah, I'll be fine," Raven said. "I filled up my canteen in town. I just need to hydrate and sweat it out. If you don't mind, I'm not sure I'm up for conversation right now."

"No worries," Kit said with a smile. "I can shut my mouth every once in a while. Especially if there's funnel cake."

"Ugh, don't remind me," Raven said, another wave of nausea washing over her. She took out her canteen and slowly sipped at it while they hiked, and after a mile or two, she fell back into the rhythm of the trail. Her headache was gradually improving, and even if it didn't, all she had to do was keep putting one foot in front of the other.

Easy.

Mindless.

THEY WALKED in silence for most of the morning. It was rare for them, but it was what Raven needed. Her canteen was empty and her stomach was finally beginning to rumble with hunger by the time they reached the Grayson Highlands. It was another long stretch of open plains with views for miles, and Raven turned around to look at Kit when they arrived on the edge of the space.

"What?" Kit asked.

"Do you know what's special about the Grayson Highlands?"

"No, what?"

"Wild ponies," Raven said. "My guidebook tells me that there are herds of them in this area, and if we're lucky, we might see a few."

"That's pretty cool," Kit said. She came up beside Raven and put her hand around her waist, then asked, "Are you feeling any better?"

"Yeah," Raven said. "I think the fog is finally starting to lift, and I'm kind of hungry."

"Do you want to stop for lunch?" Kit asked.

"Let's get to the other side of this clearing first," Raven said. "I don't want to be out here in the open at the hottest part of the day, and I'll probably appreciate that apple all the more if I'm *really* starving when I eat it."

"Fair enough," Kit said. She offered her canteen to Raven and Raven took a sip gratefully, and then she dug her phone out of her pack so that she could take pictures just in case they came across the fabled pony herds.

They kept their eyes peeled as they walked along the beaten path across the Highlands, looking in the distance for any sign of ponies. They'd been on the path for about fifteen minutes when Kit ran up beside Raven and tugged on her arm excitedly, pointing into the distance and whispering, "There!"

Raven followed her gaze and saw a pack of about a dozen short, stout ponies with long, flowing blond manes. They were gathered on a ridge about a hundred yards away and she and Kit stopped to admire them.

"There are so many," Raven said in awe. She set her pack down so she could take better pictures of them, and Kit did the same beside her.

She'd snapped about a half-dozen photos when the ponies noticed the two of them, and Kit was practically jumping up and down beside her as she said quietly, "They're coming over here!"

"Be calm," Raven said, amused at Kit's excitement. "You don't want to scare them away."

The ponies were trotting determinedly toward them and Raven wondered how close they would come. No doubt, they were used to hikers in their territory, and they didn't seem shy.

"Can I give them one of your apples?" Kit asked.

"Yeah," Raven said. "Go ahead. Just make sure to leave me one. I've been thinking about it for miles."

"I'm just going to cut one of them up and make it last," Kit said. She went over to Raven's pack and found the apples, then took out Raven's Swiss Army knife to slice it. Raven kept her camera poised while the ponies came over and Kit had to work fast to cut up the apple before the ponies completely surrounded her.

"Wow, I didn't think they'd come this close to us," Raven said. They were completely surrounded by at least six ponies, all of them vying for the treat that Kit held in her hands. She folded up the knife and tucked it back into Raven's pack, then threw a couple of apple slices over the ponies' heads to Raven.

"Here," she said. "You feed them, too."

Raven caught the apple slices with a little bit of trouble, and a couple of the ponies turned their attention to her. She laughed as they licked and nudged her in single-minded pursuit of the apple. She gave it up easily, then watched as Kit tried to manage the small herd that had surrounded her, making sure they all got equal shares of the apple and running her hand along their manes.

"They're so friendly," she said as one of them snatched an apple slice out of her hand. As soon as it moved away, another came to replace him and Kit held out another slice to it. Raven stepped back and started taking pictures, and she laughed when one of her ponies stuck by her side, licking her calves for the salt on her skin.

"This is incredible," she said.

"Yeah," Kit said. "I'm so glad we didn't stick around for the rest of Trail Days."

Kit ran out of apple slices shortly and they spent about five minutes petting their new friends, until Raven spied one of them with a whole apple clenched in its teeth.

"Hey!" she said. "Kit, he got into my pack!"

"Shoot," Kit said, trying to wade through a sea of ponies to get to it. By the time she got there, though, another one had made off with the third and final apple and the rest of the herd started to disperse, heading back to the ridgeline where they'd come from. Kit looked apologetically at Raven as she handed her pack to her.

"They ate all the apples?" Raven asked.

"Yeah," Kit said. "I must have left it unzipped when they swarmed me. I'm sorry."

Raven sat down on the trail, feeling tears threatening the back of her throat. It was ridiculous, but she was pretty sure that she was about to cry over a pony eating her afternoon snack.

"Are you okay?" Kit asked, sitting down beside her.

"I was really looking forward to that apple," Raven said, her voice going watery and her frustration levels increasing. She didn't want to be this upset over an apple, but suddenly she couldn't help herself. "Damn it."

"We'll get some more the next time we're in town," Kit said. "As many apples as you want."

"That's five days from now," Raven pointed out. She put her head in her hands and said, "I just have such a freaking headache."

"I thought it was getting better," Kit said.

"It was," Raven said. "Now it's back."

"Do you want some more of my water?" Kit asked.

Raven sighed and said, "No, you should save it. I think we're almost to a water source and I can fill up again. Let's just keep going."

"Okay," Kit said meekly. She helped Raven up and they started walking again. They weren't more than twenty yards farther along the path before Kit asked, "Did I do something wrong?"

"What?" Raven asked, surprised.

"You've been in a bad mood all day," Kit said. "I thought maybe you got sick of me, or I said or did something stupid last night while I was drunk and now you're mad at me."

Raven stopped hiking. She turned around and looked guiltily at Kit.

"No," she said at last. "I'm sorry – it's not you. It's just that I've had this nagging bad feeling ever since we ran into the guys yesterday and Dodger said I'm not a lone wolf anymore."

"Why does that bother you?" Kit asked.

"I don't know," Raven said. "It just does. It makes me worry that I'm clinging to you instead of really facing my demons out here. What if I spend the next four months falling in love with you, and then we get to Maine and figure out that two damaged strangers who live a thousand miles away from each other can't possibly make things work after they leave the trail? How *could* it work? And then I'll have to go home with the knowledge that I never actually did what I came up here to do."

"What's that?" Kit asked.

"Figure out who I *am* now," Raven said, getting emotional. She forgot about her headache and the embarrassment of crying over an apple and just let it all out. "I came here to mourn the old Raven and figure out who the new one is, and I just *can't* go home with the same baggage that I carried out here."

"You already *are* different," Kit said. "When I met you, you were so closed off and self-conscious. You were scared even though I could see how hard you were trying to put on a brave face. You were afraid to let anyone in. But you let me in, right?"

Raven shook her head. "I don't know if that was such a good idea."

Kit looked like Raven had just stabbed her in the chest. She asked, "How could you say that?"

"Tell me," Raven challenged. "Tell me how a thirty-four-year-old with no roots who's allergic to commitment can live happily ever after with a forty-five-year-old breast cancer survivor who doesn't even live in the same state."

"I don't know," Kit said, the pain written all over her face. "But I have to believe that what we've found together is worth fighting for. Are you telling me that you don't want anything to do with me after we step off this mountain for the last time?"

"No," Raven said. "That's not what I'm saying. I'm just saying that realistically, we've got a *lot* of obstacles to overcome."

"And anecdotally, I never thought I'd feel the way I do about you again," Kit said. "I thought that part of me died with Monica, but you proved me wrong. Don't push me away just because you're scared. I'm scared, too."

"You think it's worth the potential pain?" Raven asked, feeling weak and wishing they were just at a shelter already so she could get some rest. It felt like they'd hiked a hundred miles since this morning, and in reality, they were only halfway done with the day's hike.

"They don't call me Parachute for nothing," Kit said. She took Raven's hand and kissed it, and then, defeated, Raven resumed the hike. They walked side by side for a while, their hands linked, even though the trail wasn't really wide enough in this section of the path and the going was difficult.

After a while, she said, "I'm sorry. I didn't mean to pick a fight."

"It's okay," Kit said. "I'm glad you told me what was upsetting you. Do you feel any better now?"

"Not really," Raven said. "But I guess all we can do is take a leap of faith."

"You know the trail doesn't *really* have magical properties, right?" Kit asked. "I'd hate for you to spend six months of your life hiking it and walk away feeling like it was a waste of time just because you didn't walk down off of Katahdin a brand new person."

"I know," Raven said with a sigh.

Kit squeezed her hand, and they kept walking.

16

KIT

Kit had done her best to comfort Raven when she broke down on the Highlands, and as the afternoon turned into the evening, they continued walking in silent contemplation. She couldn't be sure whether her reassurances had helped Raven, but it scared the hell out of her to know that Raven was walking around with thoughts like that in her head.

Kit hadn't given a lot of thought to what would happen after they finished the trail. She just assumed that they'd think of a way to keep seeing each other, and as she gave Raven the room to think and ruminate, she started to realize how naïve that had been.

Of course it wouldn't be easy.

Kit's family was in North Carolina, and Raven's was in Illinois. Raven had a career waiting for her, and Kit was still living in her parents' house. They were both committed to this trail, and committed to each other for its duration, but would they have so much in common when they went back to their normal lives?

Would Raven even still want a girl like Kit?

She meant it when she said she wanted to try, but now she couldn't imagine what that would look like. They held hands all afternoon, like two people desperate not to drift away from each other in a vast ocean.

As darkness fell, they found shelter and cooked their evening meal. Everything went on just as it always had, and yet things felt slightly different now. Kit kept trying to lift Raven's spirits, or to calm her fears, but there were questions that neither of them could answer.

So after a day or two of quiet contemplation, they both just came to a silent agreement that there was no point in dwelling on it any longer. It didn't matter what was waiting for them at the end of the trail, or whether their relationship was just a trail romance or if there was something more to it. They just couldn't know, so they might as well embrace the uncertainty and just keep hiking.

They settled back into a comfortable routine, talking about anything and everything as they walked, mostly alone, through the long stretch of Virginia trail. They passed other people now and then, and sheltered with fellow thru-hikers most of the time. When they were alone, though, they took every opportunity they had to kiss and be close to each other, and Kit was determined to appreciate every moment she spent with Raven on the AT.

TRAIL MAGIC

IT WAS ABOUT two weeks after they'd left Damascus and Trail Days when Kit found her next opportunity to live up to her trail namesake. It was late afternoon and they'd been hiking through the forest for a couple of miles, and ahead she could hear softly churning water.

"Look," she said, squeezing Raven's hand.

"What?" Raven asked. "The bridge?"

Ahead of them, there was a long steel footbridge that would carry them over a wide, calm river. Kit smiled and said, "Don't tell me I *finally* know something that you don't about the trail."

"I know that's the James River," Raven said, looking a little confused. "And we have to cross that bridge to stay on the AT. What's the big deal?"

"That bridge is a landmark," Kit said. "And do you know the tradition for thru-hikers to do on the James River Bridge?"

Raven shook her head. "No."

"I'll give you a hint," Kit said, wrapping her arms around Raven's waist and speaking low into her ear. "It's not kissing."

She kissed Raven's neck and Raven said, unable to stop herself from smiling, "I didn't mean *no, I don't know what it is*. I meant *no, I'm not doing it*."

"Why not?" Kit asked. She gave Raven's ribs a quick tickle and Raven squirmed against her, the smile that Kit loved so much finally breaking through again.

"For one thing, it's getting late," Raven said. "If we're

wet when it gets dark, we'll have a hard time warming up again. Remember how miserable it was when we got caught in that storm?"

"No," Kit said. "All I remember is how we warmed ourselves up."

"And for another thing, we still have a couple miles to go before we camp for the night," Raven said. "We don't have time."

"This'll take ten minutes," Kit said. "I promise you won't get off schedule jumping off the James River Bridge. Don't you want to have the full Appalachian Trail experience?"

"Of course," Raven said. "That's why I'm here."

"Come on, then," Kit said, shrugging off her pack at the end of the bridge. "Jump off a bridge with me."

Raven laughed and relented, taking off her own pack and setting it down next to Kit's. They took off their shirts and hiking shoes, switching to their camp sandals. Then Raven put her hand in Kit's and held it tightly as they walked a few yards onto the long footbridge, and when Kit stopped and looked over the railing, Raven asked, "How deep do you think it is?"

The water was murky but smooth, and she couldn't see the bottom. A few ripples indicated a slow current, and the river stretched on for a long way into the distance.

"Are you afraid?" Kit asked. "I know you can swim."

"I can swim," Raven said. "But I'm not fond of the idea of jumping into shallow water and breaking my legs."

"It's not shallow," Kit said. "We're far enough away from the shore, and hikers jump in here all the time. It'll be fun."

"Okay," Raven said. "I trust you."

"Good," Kit said. She climbed over the railing and waited for Raven to join her, then took her hand again and asked, "Ready?"

"Yes," Raven said. She took a deep breath and Kit did the same, then she counted to three and they both let go of the railing and leapt off the narrow ledge.

For a moment, Kit was floating, tethered only to Raven by her hand. And then she plunged feet-first into chilly water, her head going beneath the surface and her hand never leaving Raven's. The water was much colder than Kit had anticipated, despite the summer sun warming it, and when they came back to the surface, she let out a shriek at the temperature.

"Wow," Kit said as she wiped her hair from her eyes. "That's brisk."

"It's freezing!" Raven said, but she was laughing. Kit pulled her through the water and held her close, kissing her. Then Raven broke away and said, "Come on, let's get to shore before we get hypothermia."

"Yeah, okay," Kit said. She couldn't argue – it was cold.

Raven led the way and Kit swam behind, taking Raven's hand as she helped her out of the water. They grabbed their packs and clothes, then climbed back onto the bridge where the sun was baking down on the wood slats and steel beams.

"Let's lay down in the sun for a few minutes to warm up," Raven suggested. So they stretched out in the middle of the footbridge, laying head to head and letting the afternoon sun dry them like two lizards sunning themselves on a rock.

Kit reached up and found Raven's hand, kissing it as she asked, "Was it worth it?"

"Yeah," Raven said. "Thanks for making me stop."

THAT EVENING, the shelter they stayed at was occupied by a group of hikers Kit and Raven hadn't come across yet. They all sat around their camp stoves while they made dinner and shared the usual hiker introductions – *What's your trail name? Are you thru-hiking? Where are you from?* – and Kit and Raven learned that this group had come from Waynesboro, Virginia, and were doing a southbound section hike to McAfee Knob, one of the most-recognized landmarks along the trail.

Raven and Kit had come to it four days prior, and Kit had been delighted at how much it resembled Pride Rock from the Lion King, a huge boulder jutting out from the side of the mountain and affording excellent views of the surrounding forest. She and Raven had stopped there for lunch, picnicking on the rock and taking pictures to send home to their families when they stopped in the next trail town.

Kit and Raven told their shelter mates about the other interesting things to look out for between this shelter and

McAfee Knob. Then at the end of the night, the group stayed in sleeping bags on the shelter floor while Kit and Raven set up their separate tents, not wanting to make waves by climbing into the same tiny, one-person tent in front of a bunch of strangers.

It was a lonely night, and Kit fell asleep wondering if Raven was still thinking about being a lone wolf. They had fun most days, even if the scenery got a little repetitive here and there, and sometimes the conversation lulled when they momentarily ran out of things to talk about, but Kit was still enjoying Raven's company, and she hoped Raven felt the same way.

As much as she tried to avoid the truth, she knew that things had started to feel different between her and Raven ever since they left Damascus. If it was all on account of Dodger's dumb remarks while they were all drunk, Kit would have some choice words for him the next time they crossed paths.

The next morning, Kit crawled out of her tent to find that the section hikers had already moved on and Raven was crouching over her camp stove, making them both some coffee. Kit came over and wrapped her arms around Raven, kissing her neck as she said, "I missed you last night."

"I missed you, too," Raven said. She rested her head against Kit's for a moment, then said, "We have a lot of miles to cover today. It's almost twenty miles to our next shelter at Cash Hollow Rock. Want some coffee?"

"Yeah," Kit said.

She went to retrieve her cooking pot out of her pack

and then came back and sat down in the dirt beside Raven. She handed her a protein bar and they sat in silence as they ate and drank their coffee. The sun was streaming in beams of light through the dense trees surrounding the shelter and it felt really peaceful – or else, it would have if Kit didn't have such a strong sense of foreboding.

Something had changed between them and she didn't know what to do to put things back to rights. Raven had perked up at various points when Kit was able to rouse her out of her introspective state, like on the Highlands, and again on the James River Bridge, but now she was back to the reserved, brooding state that she'd been in when Kit first met her, and she didn't like it.

"You know Dodger's full of shit, right?" she asked, and Raven looked at her with confusion.

"That's true," she said with a small laugh. "But where did that come from?"

"You seem different ever since Damascus," Kit said. "I can feel your walls going back up, closing me out. I know we only met just over a month ago and I have no right to be on the inside of those walls, but if it's all because of what Dodger said about you being a lone wolf, then you should know he's one hundred percent full of shit."

"I'm sorry," Raven said. "I'm not trying to shut you out, but it has been weighing on my mind. I *need* to be a new version of myself when I get to Katahdin and having you here is kind of confusing. It's hard to stay focused when I spend all of my time thinking about you."

"Why can't I be part of your transformation?" Kit asked. "Why do I have to be an obstacle for you to overcome?"

"Because you weren't there when *this* Raven was formed," she said. "You didn't have cancer, you didn't see how it changed me and the rest of my family. You can't possibly know what it's like."

"You're right," Kit said. "I don't know. But I know *you.*"

"How could you?" Raven asked. "We've only been hiking together for five weeks."

"Believe it or not, I can see the real you even when you're trying so hard to hide it from everyone," Kit said. Raven squirmed as soon as she said it and Kit could tell she didn't like the idea of being so visible, so she added, "For what it's worth, I don't think she needs to undergo some huge Appalachian Trail transformation. I like *this* Raven."

Raven still looked a little uncomfortable, and Kit felt bad for making her feel that way. After a minute, she finished her coffee and said, "Well, I think we should start hiking soon if we're going to get all those miles in."

"Okay," Kit said. She understood exactly what Raven was feeling right now – the overwhelming urge to keep someone at arm's length. She'd been doing that like a professional for the last five years, and the only thing she could do was be patient and give Raven time to practice relaxing the muscle that pushed people away.

They spent most of those twenty miles in silence, Kit hiking a few yards back from Raven to give her space, and in that time, Kit found that she had plenty of her own demons to wrestle with. For one thing, what was it about Raven that made her so intent on *not* being pushed away?

If it was anyone else, Kit would have been more than happy to enjoy a superficial fling in the mountains and then they could mutually push each other out of their lives when it was over. But with Raven, it felt like a part of her own soul was being pulled out of her when she made this distance between them.

They got to Cash Hollow about an hour before nightfall and found a family of section hikers already setting up camp there, or trying to. There was a pair of men bickering over an enormous tent that lay limply on the ground, and two kids sitting on a pair of tree stumps nearby, laughing at their struggle.

"Hi, there," Kit said as she and Raven came up the trail to the campsite.

"Hi," one of the adults said, turning to face them. The other man was distracted by a couple of tent poles that he couldn't quite figure out how to connect, but he looked up and smiled.

"I'm Parachute and this is Lone Wolf," Kit said as they approached. "We're thru-hiking. What about you?"

"I'm Davis," one of the men said, standing up and taking Kit's hand, then Raven's. "That's my partner, Anthony, and our kids, Mark and Sarah. We're just roughing it for the weekend."

"If we can't get this tent set up, then we're going to be roughing it at a Days Inn," Anthony said, sounding frustrated.

"Can I help you with that?" Raven asked, setting down her pack. "I'm pretty much an expert at tent set-up by now."

"Oh my god, please," Anthony said. "You have no idea how close I am to snapping these tent poles in half and walking away."

Raven laughed and said, "Don't do that, or we'll never get them right."

"I told Davis we should have set all this stuff up in the back yard before we came out here," he said, admitting defeat and handing Raven the tent poles. "He promised it wasn't difficult."

"You'll get it eventually," Raven said. "It just takes a little practice."

She set right in on the task, laying out the tent and threading the poles through it, and Kit watched for a moment, along with everyone else. Raven was made for this mountain and there was no challenge Kit hadn't seen her overcome. It gave her hope that, with a little more space, Raven would work through the emotions she'd been struggling with and come back to her.

"So, you're going all the way to Maine?" one of the kids, Mark, asked from his tree stump. He looked to be around twelve years old, and the look in his eyes said he was *very* impressed with this idea.

Kit smiled and said, "That's the idea. I didn't start in Georgia, though. I'm from North Carolina so I picked up the trail near my hometown."

"That's so cool," Mark gushed. "Did you get to pick your own trail name?"

"No," Kit said. "Lone Wolf picked it for me, and another one of our thru-hiker friends named her."

"Will you give me a trail name?" Mark asked. Beside him, his older sister rolled her eyes. She looked like she might be around fourteen or fifteen, just old enough to be greatly inconvenienced when her parents decided to drag her into the forest for a weekend.

"I will," Kit said. "But I have to get to know you a little bit, first, so I can find one that fits."

"Okay," Mark said, getting off the log. "Can I help you set up your tent? Or start a fire? We were working on that earlier and we didn't get very far."

Kit looked at the steel fire ring in the center of the campsite, where they'd gathered some sticks from the perimeter of the woods. She smiled and said, "Well, I haven't earned my bonfire merit badge yet, but I'll do my best."

She took off her pack and knelt at the edge of the fire ring, taking out all of the sticks and piling them on the dirt. Mark joined her and Davis knelt down beside them, curious to watch her work. Sarah remained casually disinterested, watching them from her tree stump simply because there was nothing better to do out here except watch a fire being built or a tent being erected.

"Some of these sticks are still kind of green," Kit said, "so they'll be harder to burn. We want to save them for once the fire is already going, and focus on dry sticks first."

She started sorting through them and Mark helped her. She surprised herself – she didn't think she even *knew* that much about starting fires, but after five weeks on the trail, camping with more experienced hikers, she must have picked some survival skills up by observation.

The pile of dry sticks they ended up with wasn't very big, so she sent Davis and Mark around the perimeter of the campsite to gather more. Kit stole a few glances at Raven, working diligently on the monster of a tent that Davis and Anthony brought as it slowly took shape. It must be at least a six-person tent, if not bigger, and she laughed as she watched it go up.

"Are you guys planning to take in boarders?" Kit asked Anthony.

"No," he said. "We just wanted to make sure everyone had room to stretch out."

"You're lucky there was even a flat area large enough to set up a tent that large," Kit said.

"Oh, crap," Davis said as he and Mark came back with an armful of sticks and branches for kindling. "Are you and Lone Wolf going to be able to set up your tents? Or tent, as the case may be?"

"It's fine. We'll probably just sleep in the shelter tonight," Kit said. That was, unless Raven felt like being alone in her tent. Kit hoped that wouldn't be the case. She added, "It's going to get dark soon, anyway. Let's get this firewood while we can still see it."

Kit showed Mark and Davis how to stack the wood in a teepee shape so it would burn easier. She stuffed a little bit of dried grass in the center and said, "Now, do you want to see the real trick to starting a fire in nature?"

"Yes!" Mark said, and even Sarah seemed intrigued from her tree stump.

Kit smiled and noticed Raven and Anthony coming over to join them around the fire, the tent set-up completed. Kit reached dramatically into her pocket and produced a lighter, which she'd grabbed from her pack while Mark was busy gathering sticks. She flicked it open to reveal a small flame, then set it to the kindling in the fire ring. Sarah rolled her eyes and Mark looked a little disappointed, but Kit just laughed. She spent a minute or two feeding more dry sticks into the fire, and when it was crackling steadily, she sat down next to Raven and put her arm around her.

"Should we start dinner before it gets too dark to see?" she asked. "I'm thinking rice tonight instead of pasta."

"Oh, let us feed you," Anthony said. "We brought salmon to cook over the fire."

"I wouldn't want to impose," Raven said. "We've got our own food."

"Please," he insisted. "As a thank-you for all your help."

"Anthony's a fantastic chef," Davis said. "If I were you, I'd take him up on the offer."

"Well, thank you," Raven said. "Can we help?"

"Nope," Anthony said. "You two just relax, and tell us more about what it's like to hike the entire Appalachian Trail."

He and Davis went over to a large plastic cooler at the edge of the campsite, which must have been a lot of trouble to pack all the way out here. They each grabbed a handle and carried it over to the fire, and while Anthony prepared the fish, Kit and Raven took turns sharing their favorite stories of the trail so far.

Kit snuggled into Raven's side and Raven melted right back into her. It was a nice night, and Davis was right – the fish was incredible.

17

RAVEN

Raven and Kit slept in sleeping bags beside each other on the platform of the shelter that night. She laid her sleeping pad sideways between them to use as a pillow, and her hips were aching from direct contact with the hard wood platform long before morning came.

Raven lay awake in the early hours before the sun rose, listening to Anthony or Davis snoring loudly inside the enormous tent that took up most of the campsite and wishing Kit had the foresight to pack a few more necessities of her own. They'd been sharing Raven's trekking poles for weeks, and as much fun as it was to sleep snuggled against each other, some nights it just wasn't practical to share one narrow sleeping pad.

Like tonight.

If Kit was going to keep hiking with her, they would *have* to go into a town that had a camping supply store and get her some more equipment to round out her pack.

Raven gave up sleeping around six in the morning

and went a little way back up the trail where they'd hiked yesterday. There were some large boulders at the top of a hill back there, looking out over the mountain ranges, and they looked peaceful. Raven found the boulders again, sitting down on them and focusing on clearing her mind for a while.

She centered all of her attention on her breath, and the feeling of the early morning mountain air filling her lungs. She listened to the breeze rustling through the trees around her and heard the birdsong as the rest of the world woke up to join her.

This was what her journey had been like in her mind. Solitude on the side of a mountain, nothing except Raven and the nature that surrounded her – that was what she'd spent twelve months picturing while she planned her trip.

She liked Kit.

She liked her so much that it was scary.

But when Raven was with her, she had no room for sitting on boulders and communing with nature, or finding herself. Every time she was near Kit, all she wanted to do was commune with *her*. She was a beautiful distraction, but she *was* a distraction.

When the boulder got too hard and uncomfortable beneath her, Raven stood up, stretched a bit and enjoyed the view, then headed back to camp. She woke Kit up with a kiss, then they quietly packed their things and prepared to head back onto the trail. Kit tore a blank page out of the back of the shelter log and left Anthony and Davis a note thanking them for dinner, and Raven looked over her shoulder to read it as she finished writing.

At the bottom of the note, Kit had printed, *P.S. – Mark, your trail name is Beaver because you're so good at finding firewood. Sarah, I know you didn't ask for one, but sometimes the trail name just finds you. You're the Queen Bee, overseeing all of us workers from your throne. Enjoy your trip, everyone!*

Raven laughed and wondered, "Do you think she'll like that?"

"It's not important to like your trail name," Kit said. "Right, Lone Wolf?"

She tucked the note under a rock on top of one of the tree stumps, and then they started the day's hike.

IT WAS a sunny June morning when they reached the Appalachian Trail Conservancy center, which marked the first 1,000 miles on the trail. Raven had been hiking for just over two months, making good time thanks to a little bit of yellow blazing here and there, and Kit was not far behind her as far as time served.

When they got to the Conservancy center, Raven paused for a moment outside the building and said, "Huh. I thought I'd feel more accomplished at this point, but it doesn't really *feel* like I've hiked a thousand miles already."

"Well, *I* can feel it," Kit said. "Forty-seven days on the trail and I can *absolutely* feel it, even if I am about a hundred and fifty miles behind you. Should we go sign the registry and get our pictures taken?"

"Yeah, definitely," Raven said.

They went inside the old stone building and found a desk with a trail volunteer sitting behind it. He gave them the registry and they both signed their trail names. Raven included the thru-hiker number that she'd been given in Georgia so that her journey could be tracked for the official records.

She and Kit spent a minute or two glancing through the book, looking for Dodger and his crew, but they hadn't signed in yet.

"They must be yellow blazing a lot," Raven said. "I bet Eagle Scout is not happy about that."

"I'd say we should invite him to hike with us next time we see him," Kit said, "but I'm not sure Break Time and Dodger would survive without him."

Raven laughed, and then the volunteer took the book back and said, "You're halfway there. How does it feel?"

"It doesn't feel real," Raven said.

"Speak for yourself," Kit interjected. "*I* feel like I've hiked two Appalachian Trails by now."

The volunteer took out an old Polaroid camera from beneath the counter and had Raven and Kit stand together against a wall. Kit put her arm around Raven's shoulder and he snapped the photo, then they stood around for a few minutes waiting for it to develop.

"We look good," Kit said, grinning at Raven when they saw it.

"Wow," Raven said, taking the photo and studying

herself. She had to agree with Kit – they both looked tan and lean, their shoulder muscles defined and their bodies optimized from weeks of hiking. She almost didn't recognize herself. She watched with pride as the volunteer pinned their photo on a wall with over a hundred others.

IT WAS ONLY about a week later when they came across their next landmark. First they'd hit the 1,000-mile marker, and now, one day before Raven's seventieth day on her adventure, they came to the official half-way mark of the Appalachian Trail. It was located within Pine Grove National Park, and as they hiked up to the 1089.3-mile marker, Raven said to Kit, "Are you ready for the next AT tradition?"

"Yes," Kit said enthusiastically. Then she smiled and asked, "What is it?"

"The half-gallon challenge," Raven said. "Pretty much what it sounds like. Half a gallon of ice cream, and you get as much time as you need to finish it. If you get to the bottom of the tub, you win."

"What do I win?" Kit asked. "A bellyache?"

"Yeah, and bragging rights," Raven said, smiling. She led Kit into the park, which also had a lake, showers, and some other amenities that were mostly geared toward day hikers and families but which the thru-hikers could use as well. They went to a little general store, the Pine Grove Furnace Store, where they could pick from a variety of different ice cream flavors.

Kit asked Raven, "You up for it?"

"It's part of the trail experience, right?" Raven asked. "Let's do it."

Raven picked rocky road, while Kit went for Neapolitan because she said if there were three flavors to work her way through, she wouldn't get sick of any one flavor as fast.

"That's probably smart," Raven conceded. They bought their half-gallons from a clerk behind the counter, who handed them each a plastic spoon as well. Then they took their tubs of ice cream out to a row of picnic benches on a brick-paved area outside of the store. Kit and Raven were not the only ones out there – there was a trio of other hikers, two guys and a girl, powering through the last few bites of their own Half-Gallon Challenges, and they went over to observe for a moment.

One of the guys had already finished, while his friends were working steadily toward the bottoms of their tubs. Kit pulled the lid off her Neapolitan ice cream and started working on the chocolate while she asked him, "How long did it take you?"

"Twenty-two minutes," he said proudly. "These two have been belaboring it for almost forty, though."

"You guys are almost there," Kit said, cheerleading them. The girl smiled, but her friend looked like he wasn't in the mood for camaraderie and Kit just laughed.

"What have we gotten ourselves into?" Raven asked.

"Join us if you want," the guy said. "I'm Bear and these are my friends, Stream Hopper and Beans."

Kit and Raven introduced themselves, then sat down

at their table. Raven started in on her tub of rocky road, and Kit and Raven were less than a quarter of the way through their own challenges when Stream Hopper and Beans finally got to the bottoms of their tubs.

They both looked somewhat miserable, but Bear just clapped them on their backs and said, "Okay, let's go claim our prize!"

"What is it?" Kit asked.

"I'll show you," he said. He and his friends went back into the store, while Kit and Raven focused on the task at hand. The ice cream was cold and creamy, a treat that they weren't used to and which went down easily for a while.

By the time the trio came back out of the store about ten minutes later, Stream Hopper and Beans both looked a little better and Bear came over to the picnic table and set down a little wooden spoon between Kit and Raven. It had *Member of Half-Gallon Club* stamped on it in red ink, and Raven let out a hearty laugh.

"That's it?" she asked. "That's what we're all putting ourselves through frozen dairy hell for?"

"It's gotta be light enough to store in your pack," Bear said with a shrug. "Hey, it's all about the experience, right?"

"Damn right," Kit said. She'd been methodically working her way through her tub by flavor. The chocolate was all gone and she was working on the strawberry ice cream now. "I don't know about you, but I'm having fun."

"Tell me that when you're on the vanilla," Raven said with a chuckle.

"Well, we're gonna hit the trail," Bear said. "Good luck!"

Raven and Kit watched them walk away, slow and sluggish but holding their heads high. Raven and Kit spent almost an hour at that picnic table, slowly working their way through their tubs as the ice cream grew soupier in the sun. Kit slowed down once she got to the vanilla, letting it melt until it became the consistency of a milkshake, then she set down her plastic spoon and tipped the whole tub toward her mouth, drinking the last third of her ice cream.

Raven had to admit that was a pretty clever idea.

By the time she got to the bottom of her own tub, her belly was full and she was eager to march with Kit back into the store to claim her little wooden spoon. Once she had it in her hand, she looked at Kit and said, "You know what? That does feel good."

Kit laughed and said, "Please don't tell me you feel more accomplished at pounding a half-gallon of ice cream than you did when you signed the register at the half-way mark."

Raven grinned at that and said, "I just might. I'm sure the accomplishment will sink in eventually, but it's hard to forget that there are another thousand miles waiting for us. At least I can say that the ice cream challenge is done."

Kit led Raven down to the lake and they spent an hour with their feet in the water, cooling down and digesting their ice cream before continuing on the trail. Raven called her parents and sent Annabel a short video that Kit had taken of Raven conquering her tub of rocky road, and then she lent the phone to Kit to call home.

She listened in, trying not to eavesdrop too much, as Kit glanced over at Raven and said with a smile on her lips, "Yeah, Mom. I'm having a *really* good time."

18
KIT

That night, they had a shelter all to themselves again. The middle part of the trail was the least-trafficked since a certain portion of their fellow northbound hikers had thrown in the towel and they hadn't quite reached the point where they would begin to encounter a lot of southbounders crossing their path.

Kit and Raven enjoyed the solitude, preparing a light meal since they were both still overwhelmed with the richness of their afternoon treat, and then when it was time to go to bed, Raven erected her tent and led Kit inside.

She lay down on the sleeping pad and pulled Kit down on top of her. The moon was large in the sky outside and it shone through the nylon sides of the tent, illuminating Raven's soft complexion. Kit tucked her hair behind her ear and kissed her, saying, "I'm so glad that I found you."

"I think I'm the one who found you," Raven

answered. She circled her hands around Kit's hips and it felt so good to be in her arms.

"Are you glad?" Kit asked.

"Yes," Raven said. Then she kissed her again and slid her hands beneath Kit's shirt.

They made love to the low moan of the wind through the pine trees, slowly and carefully, savoring every moment that they had with each other. Kit was starting to really feel at home when her body was pressed against Raven's, their curves fitting together and Raven's lips always tasting sweet. But even with her hand between Raven's thighs, watching her arch her back in pleasure and listening to the animal moans and groans of her pleasure, Kit could feel the tiniest sliver of distance between them. A narrow wall that they both did their best not to acknowledge, but which neither of them was willing to tear down.

Giving up her life to be on a mountain for two months with a woman she just met was nothing compared to the bravery it took to fall in love.

THE NEXT DAY, Kit and Raven hiked through the Rock Maze. It was a half-mile of fallen boulders the size of cars and even small houses, and the two of them had to scramble up and over, through tight spaces, and even underneath the massive stones.

It had rained lightly in the night and the whole forest smelled damp and musky. This also meant that the boulders were slick, and many of them were covered in moss that made the going all the more treacherous. When Kit and Raven got to the Maze, Raven put her hand on the surface of a rock to test it and said, "It's really slick. We'll have to be careful."

"It'll be fine," Kit said. "Except I'm not sure how much tread I've got left on my boots."

"Let me see," Raven said.

Kit sat on one of the boulders, the moss starting to dampen her shorts, and Raven inspected her boots. Kit had been wearing them for the last fifty-odd days and the glue was beginning to disintegrate, the soles separating from the rest of the shoe.

"How come you didn't say your shoes were falling apart?" Raven asked. She seemed a little annoyed by this development, and Kit didn't understand why.

"What difference does it make?" Kit asked, taking her foot back and standing up.

"Those can't be waterproof anymore," Raven said. "Are you walking around in wet socks all day?"

"Sometimes," Kit said with a shrug. "Isn't that just the price of hiking, though?"

"You're going to get blisters and sores and all kinds of other problems," Raven said. "Not to mention the fact that you're right – you have almost no treads left, and we're coming up on some of the rockiest, roughest parts of the trail."

Kit laughed and said, "The *whole trail* is the roughest part of the trail."

"No," Raven corrected. "It's not. You're going to step

on a sharp rock and hurt yourself one of these days, or slip off a wet boulder and break your leg. We need to get you new boots as soon as possible."

"Okay," Kit said. "How the heck do we do that? We're out in the middle of the Pennsylvania wilderness."

"There's nothing we can do about it today," Raven agreed. "We're resupplying in Wind Gap next week. That'll probably be our best hope of finding a sporting goods store to get everything you need. Hey, maybe you can finally stop borrowing my trekking poles then."

Kit laughed and said, "I'm sorry I didn't spend an entire year packing like you."

She was joking, but there was truth in it. Raven looked a little irritated, but she let it go and said with a smile, "If you had, we never would have met."

"That's true," Kit said. "Now are we going to climb some boulders or what?"

She grinned and climbed up onto the first one, hefting herself forward despite the weight of her pack trying to pull her backward. Raven gave her a push and then Kit took her hand to pull her up. She pulled Raven into a quick embrace, kissing her, and chose not to tell her just how slippery the rock felt beneath her inadequately treaded hiking boots.

They picked their way across the boulders, over and under fallen rocks that had been there since the glaciers moved them. Kit moved faster than Raven, treating the boulders like a playground while Raven came slowly and carefully behind her.

"Watch your step," Raven cautioned. "There are a lot of rattlesnakes in Pennsylvania."

"All the more reason to quickly get back *out* of Pennsylvania," Kit said, looking over her shoulder and shooting Raven a smile. "But I guess that's not going to happen any time soon."

"Nope," Raven agreed. "We've got another seven days before we get to the New Jersey part of the trail. And we've got to get through Dante's Inferno before we can close the book on PA."

"What's that?" Kit asked.

"A fifteen-mile hike through a waterless wasteland," Raven said. "There was a zinc factory in the area about a hundred years ago and it polluted the land until nothing could grow there except for weeds and rattlesnakes. It's the last landmark before we leave the state."

"I can't wait," Kit said, rolling her eyes even though she didn't turn around for Raven to see it.

"Just be careful with your shoes," Raven said. "You don't want to spend a whole day hiking through a rattlesnake playground in your camp sandals."

"No," Kit agreed. "I do not. These rocks, on the other hand, are a lot of fun."

She slid down a great big boulder covered in moss, letting it stain the back of her pants because they were wet anyway. She turned around and waited for Raven, then caught her on her way down.

19

RAVEN

The day they hiked Dante's Inferno, it was hot and dry. Kit and Raven both filled their canteens at the shelter that morning, and sipped conservatively from them until they reached the Inferno. It was a wide-open part of the trail, with pine trees on either side of a long corridor leading them up a gradual slope covered in rocks of varying size and pointiness.

Raven was worried about Kit's hiking boots. She'd been wearing them for two full months by now and they weren't the best boots for the Appalachian Trail in the first place. Raven, on the other hand, had purchased four different pairs of trail runner sneakers and packed them in her drop boxes to be replaced at even intervals. Spending eight hours a day on your feet had a way of breaking down even the sturdiest of shoes, and Kit's boots were much worse for the wear.

"Here," Raven said, taking her trekking poles out of her pack and handing one of them to Kit. "Use this to steady yourself, and to look for rattlesnakes. It's hot out, so they'll be curled up in the shady spots between the rocks. You'll much rather find them with a trekking pole than your boot."

"Is it true they don't strike above the ankle?" Kit asked. "I heard that on a nature show once."

"I wouldn't bet on it," Raven said. "Best to just avoid being struck at in the first place."

"You're making me nervous," Kit said. "How many rattlesnakes do you think there are out there?"

They both looked at the long stretch of rocky terrain ahead of them. They'd be picking their way across it for most of the day, and it would be slow going.

"Enough to be listed as a hazard in the trail literature," Raven said. "Let's just get started. The sooner we do, the sooner we'll be safe on the other side. Then we can rest up for a day in Wind Gap as our reward."

"Well, that part sounds good," Kit said. She extended the telescopic trekking pole, locking it in place, and Raven did the same with hers. They started walking side by side and Raven wobbled a bit as she tried to balance on the uneven rocks. This would have been much easier with both of her trekking poles in hand, and she was suddenly cursing herself for not insisting that Kit stock up on all the little things she'd neglected to bring for herself when they'd been in trail towns along the way.

It wasn't that big a deal until now to share, and Raven rather liked the fact that having only one single-person sleeping pad between them meant that Kit slept most nights with her arm and her thigh thrown around Raven.

She liked to snuggle against Kit in the night, protected from the unknown dangers in the darkness beyond their tent.

But it would be nice to have full use of her own equipment sometimes.

"Do you actually think we're going to see rattlesnakes?" Kit asked. She was already starting to hike ahead of Raven, hopping quickly from rock to rock.

"Slow down," Raven warned. "Check your footing before you step. Yes, I think it's pretty likely that we're going to see a couple of rattlesnakes. If we're lucky, they'll be sunning themselves on rocks far away from us."

Raven kept her eyes on the ground as she walked, looking for loose or sharp rocks, crevices where snakes could be lying in wait, and listening for the telltale rattle of their tails. Meanwhile, Kit jumped from rock to rock as if she were playing a lively game of *the floor is made of lava,* or in this case, *the ground is made of rattlesnakes*.

Raven got tired of chastising her, and maybe she was being a little overly cautious. Thousands of hikers crossed this portion of the trail every year without incident, so there was no reason to think the two of them would be any different.

She relaxed for a while, resisting the urge to nag while she watched Kit hop her way across the Inferno. Raven told Kit about Wind Gap, which she knew from her research was one of the bigger trail towns they would come across on their journey. They decided that tonight, they'd treat themselves to something a little more luxurious than usual and find a good steakhouse for dinner.

Raven was just salivating at the thought of a big pile of creamy mashed potatoes, poking her trekking pole in between the rocks in front of her as she had been, when Kit yelped ahead of her.

"What's wrong?" Raven asked, snapping her head up to look.

Kit stumbled and fell across the rocks, then screamed as a rattlesnake darted out from a crevice. Raven could hear its tail shaking angrily and Kit scrambled across the rocks just as it struck the sole of her boot.

"Be careful!" Raven yelled. "Look where you're going!"

She was watching the rocks where Kit was putting her hands, scrambling terrified away from the rattlesnake and praying that there weren't more of them nearby.

"I'm a little preoccupied, here," Kit said. Raven could hear the terror in her voice and she hopped as fast as she could across the rocks toward her, still checking her footing before each step. There would be no point in sacrificing her own safety to get to Kit if they *both* ended up with rattlesnake bites.

Kit threw her trekking pole like a javelin at the rattler and the side of the pole hit the snake, then stuck into the ground at an odd angle. The snake slithered back to safety beneath the rocks, and Raven finally got to Kit, helping her to her feet.

"Are you okay?" she asked as she led Kit, limping slightly, further away from the rocks where the snake had retreated.

"That was terrifying," Kit said, slightly out of breath.

She brushed off her bare legs, which were dirty from scrambling over the rocks. "I rolled my ankle."

"The snake didn't pierce your shoe, though?" Raven asked. "Let me see your foot."

Kit obliged, leaning on Raven and lifting up her foot so they could inspect the sole of her boot. It was intact, and Raven felt relief washing over her.

"Holy crap, that scared me," she said.

"You?" Kit asked, laughing. "I nearly pissed myself."

"Stay here," Raven said. She handed Kit her trekking pole to steady herself, then walked cautiously across the rocks to retrieve her other pole. She pulled it out of the dirt, then frowned. The way Kit had thrown it, it must have twisted when it was lodged in the ground. The aluminum was bent and it would obviously snap if either of them put their weight on it. She rejoined Kit, muttering, "It's broken."

"Shit," Kit said. "I'm sorry."

"I warned you about the snakes," Raven said. "I told you to test your footholds before you stepped."

"I was," Kit said. Raven rolled her eyes. She *wasn't*. Raven had been watching her. "I'll buy you a new set in Wind Gap, okay?"

"Yeah, okay," Raven said. She was distracted, trying to retract the broken pole so at least she wouldn't have to carry it fully extended all the way out of the Inferno. But the aluminum was pinched and it wasn't going to retract. In a moment of frustration, Raven snapped the broken piece of the pole off and tucked it into her pack, then retracted what was left of it. Then she shook off her irritation because there was no point in holding onto that, too, and asked, "Can you put weight on your ankle?"

Kit tested it out, stepping from rock to rock and then coming back to Raven. "Yeah. I think the hiking boot protected it."

"Okay," Raven said. "Let's get out of here. You follow me this time."

She took up the lead, forcing Kit to slow down and go at her pace as she tested each crevice and rock with her remaining trekking pole before stepping forward. It was slow going, but she wasn't about to risk another run-in with a rattlesnake.

After a minute or two, Kit said, "I'm sorry I didn't listen to you."

Raven didn't turn around. She just said, "It's okay. We all make mistakes."

THEY GOT into Wind Gap late that evening, just as the sun was starting to set. They were both starving and exhausted, but Kit insisted that they go to the sporting goods store right away and replace Raven's trekking poles.

"It can wait," Raven tried to object, but Kit insisted.

"I want to make it right," Kit said. "I broke them and I'm going to buy you a new set. And I'll treat you to dinner for the trouble, okay?"

"You don't have to do that," Raven said. "Replacing the poles will be plenty."

"I insist," Kit said. "I want to do that for you."

Raven sighed, and when she saw that Kit would not be dissuaded, she agreed. They went to the sporting goods store and bought two sets of trekking poles – one for Raven and one, finally, for Kit – as well as a new pair of hiking boots to replace Kit's broken-down old ones. Kit changed into them right there in the store and wore them outside, and then they went down the street to the motel that Raven had made reservations at when she was back in Illinois.

The whole time, she felt guilty about the fact that Kit was being so nice to her because Raven had been moody and quiet all afternoon. She just couldn't shake the irritation she felt at how flippant Kit had been about the rattlesnake incident, and it was frustrating that Raven couldn't make her see how important it was to take that hike seriously.

There could have been really serious repercussions, and the truth was that they'd gotten lucky.

They went to Raven's motel room and set down their packs, along with their new equipment. Kit suggested they freshen up before dinner, and even though she was starving, Raven agreed that was a good idea.

"Come on," Kit said, reaching for Raven's hand. "Shower with me."

"No," Raven said, taking her hand back. "I'm exhausted. I don't think I have the energy."

Kit frowned, but she left Raven on the bed as she went into the bathroom. Raven flopped backward and listened as the water came on, and Kit started singing in the shower like she always did. Carefree Kit. She had no idea why her brush with the rattlesnake bothered Raven so much.

She just didn't seem to be taking any part of their trip seriously anymore. At first, Kit's approach to the trail had been equal parts amusing and terrifying, and just charming enough to make Raven curious to know more about her. But lately, Raven was beginning to see that attitude leaking into their relationship as well. Kit was building walls between them again and Raven couldn't ignore what she knew about Kit.

She didn't let people in. She ran when things got serious. She was afraid to love because it wasn't worth the pain.

What made Raven think that a few months on the Appalachian Trail could change Kit if it couldn't change Raven?

She closed her eyes and listened to Kit's voice, muffled by the running water. After a few minutes, she drifted off. She was so tired from being in the hot sun all day, from the careful hiking that the Inferno required, and from trying to be a new Raven who didn't really exist yet. She'd never given that version of herself room to incubate – she'd just thrown herself into a relationship with Kit instead. Kit was amazing, but she was unavailable and she was keeping Raven from finding herself out here.

THE NEXT TIME Raven opened her eyes, it was to the sensation of cool, damp hair tickling her temples. She looked up and saw Kit leaning over her, those big blue eyes like impenetrable oceans.

"Hey," she said softly. "Shower's free."

"Okay," Raven said. Kit leaned further over to kiss her, but Raven ducked around her and sat up. "I'm going to hop in and then we can eat."

She was halfway to the bathroom when Kit called, "Wait. What's wrong?"

Raven turned around and lied. "Nothing."

Kit came over to her. She was wearing a motel towel wrapped around her chest and the soft terry cloth brushed against Raven's fingertips as Kit stood close to her and said, "I don't believe you."

"I don't know what to say," Raven answered. "I'm just tired and hungry, and kind of frustrated."

"Are you still mad at me about the trekking poles?" Kit asked.

"No," Raven said. "It was never about the trekking poles."

"What, then?"

Raven sighed. If Kit wanted a fight, Raven was too tired to keep her temper in check and avoid it. She looked into Kit's eyes and said, "You aren't taking it seriously."

"The Inferno?"

"All of it!" Raven said, exasperated. "You show up here with insufficient equipment and no plan. You expect everyone else to jump in and keep you out of trouble-"

"I thought you *liked* that about me," Kit interrupted, but Raven talked over her.

"You don't listen to me, you make me fall for you, and I can just *tell* you're getting ready to break my heart as soon as we get to the end of the trail," she said. "You haven't changed."

"*You* haven't even *tried* to change," Kit shot back. "You keep saying that you came out here to become a new woman and all you do is stubbornly cling to your itineraries and your plans and your rigid, solitary ways."

"I haven't had the *time* to change," Raven said. "I met you three weeks into my trip and we've been attached at the hip ever since. I can't catch my breath around you, let alone find any time for introspection or self-discovery."

"I don't understand why you think you need to be *alone* to do that!" Kit said. She took a step away, looking like she might cry or punch a wall, and then she turned back to Raven and said, "I've known who you are since the first day I met you, and you just can't believe that anyone would care about you or love you because you're so wrapped up in the idea of being damaged and needing to be fixed. You're not broken, Raven!"

"I am!" Raven shouted. "And you don't know me, because if you did, you wouldn't be standing here right now. I could have died! I was sick and I could have died!"

She slid down the wall, suddenly feeling like there wasn't enough oxygen in the room. It all hit her at once. Kit had opened the floodgates and now it was all pouring in, suffocating her. She gasped for breath and when Kit reached for her, Raven shoved her away.

"I spent the last three years trying to reassure everyone in my life that I was okay, that I was strong, and I wasn't going anywhere," Raven said. "When was it *my* turn to be reassured? I came out here to find a way to be okay with that, and instead I found a woman who can't love me because she's terrified that if she loves someone, they'll die on her. That's great."

Kit sat down hard on the edge of the bed, putting her hands on her knees and letting Raven's words sink in.

After a long moment of silence, Kit said, "So, I can't love you because I'm afraid that you're fragile, and you can't stop being fragile unless I leave you alone to build all those walls around yourself. Did I get that right?"

"We're broken in uncomplimentary ways," Raven said.

"Maybe so," Kit answered.

They both thought about that for a few minutes, and then Raven asked, "So what do we do now?"

"I guess this is the end for me," Kit said. "I always said I'd hike as long as you'd have me. Turns out the end of the line is Wind Gap."

"You're going to stop hiking?" Raven asked, alarmed.

"I've been on the trail much longer than I thought I would be," Kit said. She got up from the bed and went into the bathroom, changing out of the towel and back into her clothes. Raven stood up when she came back into the room, and watched with a sense of dread as Kit gathered her pack and her shopping bag from the outdoor shop. She looked into it and said, "Shame we didn't have this conversation *before* I bought the shoes and trekking poles."

"You can't just *leave*," Raven said, her brain switching over to practical matters. "It's eight o'clock at night. How are you going to get home?"

"I'll hitch," Kit said.

"Don't do that," Raven begged her. "You could end up with a crazy person."

"Well I'm certainly not going to take a cab all the way back to North Carolina," Kit said. "And I can't stay here anymore."

"You could get a separate motel room," Raven suggested.

"Why bother?" Kit asked. "It's not like I'll sleep tonight anyway."

Raven went over to Kit, stopping her before she could run out of the room. She always knew Kit would run away from her one day. She put her hand on Kit's arm and said, "If you're going to hitchhike in the middle of the night, then you at least have to call your parents before you go. Let them know you're coming so they know where you are."

She dug her phone out of her pack and handed it to Kit, who looked like she was fighting back tears.

She took the phone and said, "You worry too much."

Then she went into the bathroom and closed the door. Raven could hear her voice, muffled, but not her words. Then a couple of minutes later, Kit came out and handed Raven the phone.

"Thank you," she said. She let out a long sigh and,

after an obvious internal struggle, she pulled Raven into a tight hug. Raven nearly burst into tears, and Kit said over her shoulder, "It's been really nice getting to know you, Lone Wolf. Good luck out there."

"Goodbye, Parachute," was all Raven could manage. Her throat was tight with tears.

Kit let go of her and went over to the door, and just before she closed it, she gave Raven one last look and said, "I hope you find what you're looking for."

Then she was gone and Raven was all alone in a small, cheap motel room on the edge of Pennsylvania. She sank down to the floor right where she stood, leaning her back up against the bedspread, and cried.

How could something that seemed so inevitable hurt this much?

20

KIT

Kit left the motel room and started walking. She didn't have a clear aim at that moment, except to put some distance between herself and Raven. Her stomach was rumbling, so her feet led her to a fast food restaurant on the other side of the street. She bought a burger and fries and then went outside to sit on a bench and enjoy the breeze on her face. She ate mechanically, trying not to think about the argument she and Raven had just had.

It came out of nowhere, and yet it had been building for weeks.

When a semi-trailer pulled up in front of the restaurant and put on its air break with a loud whoosh, Kit stood up. A middle-aged man with a suntanned face got out of the truck, and he had a friendly smile when he noticed Kit with her pack and her shopping bag.

"Hey, there," he said. He spoke with a southern

accent and Kit wondered how far he was driving that truck. "You need a lift back to the trail, little lady?"

"No, I'm done with the trail," Kit said, shoving the last of her French fries to the side of her cheeks. "Are you going south? I'm trying to get to North Carolina."

"That's a long way from here," he said. "Are you in trouble?"

"No trouble," Kit said. "I was hiking the AT and I just don't want to do it anymore. My parents are expecting me back home in Asheville."

"Well, I'm on my way to Atlanta," the man said. "Asheville's a little out of my way, but I can get you closer than you are now."

"Really?" Kit asked. "Thank you so much."

"I'm starving, so you'll just have to wait for a minute while I refuel," the man said, and Kit nodded eagerly.

"Let me buy your dinner," she said. "It's the least I can do."

"Nah," he answered. "I appreciate it, but I'll manage. Wait here and I'll be out in a few."

Kit sat back down on the bench while he went inside the restaurant. She glanced back across the street at the motel but Raven hadn't come out. The curtains were drawn and Kit hoped she'd taken the time to draw the chain across the door. Wind Gap was a much bigger city than the other trail towns they'd come across, and this trucker seemed like a decent guy, but she wasn't sure about the rest of the town's inhabitants.

The man took longer than Kit expected to get his food, and she was just feeling itchy, wondering if she should run back across the street and beg Raven to keep trying, when he reappeared. He was carrying a large sack of food and a Styrofoam cup and he gestured to the truck.

"Hop in," he said. "My name's Angus, by the way."

He extended one callused hand to Kit as they walked across the parking lot to his truck, and for a split second, she was about to introduce herself as Parachute. Then she shook the word out of her head and said, "Kit. Thanks again for helping me out."

"Gets lonely on the road," Angus said. "It's nice having someone to talk to here and there. You can put your pack in the sleeper area in the back if you want."

She climbed into the cab while Angus went around to the driver's side, and glanced into the small sleeper cabin behind the seats. Instead, she decided to keep her pack between her feet, and then Angus threw the truck into gear and they lurched back onto the road. Angus dug into his dinner and Kit just watched the road as they rolled out of Wind Gap.

She might never see Raven again. Probably wouldn't. She didn't know Raven's phone number, or where she lived in Chicago, and Raven had been right about a lot of things when she was finally honest with Kit about how she was feeling. It was naïve to think their relationship was anything more than a momentary trail romance.

Goodbye, Raven, Kit thought as they turned onto the dark highway.

"I don't mean to be rude, but did the trail whoop ya?" Angus asked when he'd polished off his burger. Kit gave him a confused look and he nodded to the pack between her feet. "You're a thru-hiker, right?"

"Kind of," Kit said.

She was trying to find the right words to explain her situation when Angus carried on. He must have thought she'd taken offense, because he hastily added, "I drive up and down the East Coast about a hundred times a year and I like to pick up hikers because they always got interesting stories to tell. Most of the time they just wanna ride into town, but sometimes I pick up people who thrown in the towel. It's nothing to be ashamed of – that trail sounds like a beast."

"That's not what I'm doing," Kit said, although Angus wasn't too far off-base. She softened up and said, "I was never planning on hiking the whole thing. I actually made it a lot farther than I thought I would. I thought I'd hike for a week, maybe two, and then get bored and go home. Instead, I've been out here for two whole months."

"You catch the trail fever?" Angus asked. "I never hiked it myself but I hear it's kind of a rush."

"It is, but mostly I just kept hiking because I met someone," Kit said. Then she hurried to add, "It didn't work out, though."

"Trail love," Angus said, nodding like he'd seen *that* a hundred times before, too. He reached for his cup and took a long sip, then said sympathetically, "Yup, the AT sure knows how to break hearts."

"Wish I'd known that before I came," Kit said. She tried to smile to lighten the mood, but it didn't work and Angus was kind enough to let her wallow for a minute.

Then he said, "Don't worry. If you're feeling bad, I'm sure your fella is, too. Maybe you can reconnect with him once you both have a chance to breathe a bit."

Kit opened her mouth to correct Angus's pronouns, then decided it was both better and easier not to. What difference did it make, anyway? She and Raven were finished whether she liked it or not.

"I don't think so," she said. "Anyway, it's probably for the best. I'm not great with commitment, and we're from totally different parts of the country. One more failed relationship averted."

"That's one way to think about it," Angus said. "You want some of these fries? My eyes were bigger than my stomach."

Kit grabbed a couple out of the bag on the console between them, and then they moved on to more cheerful conversation topics. Angus turned out to be pretty good road tripping partner, and he gave Kit a rare break from talking, proving to be an even bigger chatterbox than she was.

"I'm not really the type to sit alone in silence," he said after a few miles of small talk. "I'd probably lose my mind if I didn't have people to talk to."

"I would have thought that's a personality requirement for long-haul truck drivers," Kit said. "How'd you get into this work?"

"Accident and circumstance, just like how pretty much everyone else gets their jobs," he said. "I had this girlfriend in high school, Rita. God, she was beautiful and popular – way too good for me, but for some reason she liked me. After graduation, she ended up pregnant, and all I had to take care of her and the baby was a high school diploma. There was a trucking company down the road from our apartment, so one day I walked in and asked for an application. They hired me and it paid the bills pretty good, only the hell of it was my paychecks saw Rita and my son more than I did. It's a hard life, being on the road all the time, and we just weren't cut out for being a family."

"What happened?" Kit asked quietly. She wondered if she was prying too much, but Angus seemed to want to tell her, so she let him.

"It was always a long shot. Who actually ends up with their high school sweetheart?" he asked. "We made it about five years, and then I came home after a run one time to find her packing my bags for me. She said she found some other guy who kept her company while I was on the road, and she wanted to be with him now. My boy barely knew who I was cuz I was never home, and Rita was leaving me, and at that point I couldn't see much reason to get off the road. Been driving ever since."

"What about your son?" Kit asked. "Do you still see him?"

"Not since he was eight," Angus said.

He flipped down his sun visor and pulled a photo from it, then passed it to Kit. She tilted the photo toward the window to use the street lamps to look at it. The kid was cute, with a bowl cut and a slight gap in his front teeth, sitting proudly on top of a blue bicycle.

"That's Billy. I bought him that bike," Angus said.

"Never got to watch him ride it, though. Rita sent me that picture. He'll be twenty-three years old this year. I used to send him postcards from my route, but then I got to thinking, how many postcards from Richmond, Virginia, does a kid need?"

He chuckled at this, but Kit could hear the pain in it as she handed the photograph back and Angus carefully tucked it under the visor again.

"Now I just send him money on Christmas and his birthday," he said. "Best I can do. His stepdad's a good man, from what I can tell."

"I bet he'd like to get a postcard from Richmond," Kit said. "Are we going to pass through there on the way down south?"

"Yeah," Angus said. "But it's gonna be around two in the morning. Not sure I can get ahold of a postcard at that hour."

"It wouldn't hurt to try," Kit said.

They changed the subject again after another few minutes. The bag of French fries was depleted and Angus was reaching the bottom of his cup of soda, and Kit was beginning to feel tired in the very core of her being. She and Raven had a very early start this morning, the rocky terrain of the Inferno had sapped a lot of her energy, and if she were still on the trail, she would have climbed into the tent and curled up next to Raven at least an hour ago as the sun was going down.

She listened lazily as Angus told her about life on the road, the different types of hitchhikers he encountered, and the challenges of attempting to deliver his loads in the middle of a union strike a few years back. He'd been detained at weigh station when a couple union boys went out there with a couple of telephone poles. While Angus's truck was on the scales, they laid the poles across both sides of the weigh station ramp and trapped him there all day long.

Kit was yawning by the end of this story, trying to lock her jaws to keep from being obvious about it, but when Angus noticed, he didn't take offense.

"You must be exhausted," he said. "How many miles you say you hiked?"

"About eleven hundred in all," Kit said.

"Hoo boy," Angus said. "Well, if the sandman's calling you can use the sleeper cabin. The bed's surprisingly comfortable and I'll be fine by myself up here for a while."

"Are you sure?" Kit asked. "I don't want to take advantage of your hospitality."

"Yeah, I don't mind," Angus said. "I'm just grateful for the company."

"Okay," Kit said, unbuckling her seatbelt.

This was something that Raven would have yelled at her for, and probably her parents and Sam, too – getting into the sleeper cabin of some guy she barely knew. Angus seemed like a good guy, though, and they'd been on the road for about two hours already. If he was going to try something sinister, she didn't know why he would have waited so long.

Her eyelids were growing heavy, so she decided to embrace her Parachute nature once again. She said,

"Thank you. I really appreciate this. Wake me up in Richmond?"

"Sure," Angus said.

Kit crawled into the sleeper cabin, which was really just a narrow space with a mattress behind the seats. She turned toward the back wall so the light from the street lamps wouldn't bother her, and with the motion of the truck rocking her gently, she was asleep almost instantly.

THE NEXT TIME Kit opened her eyes, the truck had come to a stop and she felt Angus's hand on her shoulder. She turned and wiped the sleep from her eyes. The yellow light from a parking lot lamp shone through the window, and Angus was looking at her.

"Hey," he said softly. "We're in Richmond. Check it out."

He passed her a couple of postcards and she held them up to the light and smiled. She handed them back, asking, "Are you going to send them to your son?"

"One of them," he said, giving the other back to Kit. "I think you should send the other one to your hiking partner, wherever his next stop is. I bet he'll be happy to hear from you."

"Maybe," Kit said. She didn't want to go into all the details about why Raven probably wouldn't want to hear from her again, nor did she want to think about them herself. She accepted the postcard, though, and asked, "What time is it?"

"'Bout two-thirty," Angus said. "You can keep sleeping. I just figured you might wanna hit the head while we're at a rest stop."

"Oh, yeah that's a good idea," Kit said. She sat up and Angus moved out of the way to allow her to crawl back over the center console into the passenger seat. She went to the restroom, taking a few minutes to stretch her legs because sitting in one place for so long felt unnatural to her after such a long time on the trail. Then she climbed back into the truck and asked, "So maybe you can drop me in Rocky Mount when we get to North Carolina? That way you don't have to get off 95 and I can hopefully hitch another ride over to Asheville from there."

"It's going to be four-thirty in the morning if I drive straight from here to Rocky Mount," Angus said. "I hate to think of the type of person you'd find to give you a ride at that hour."

"I found you, right?" Kit asked. "I'll be fine. I'm a pretty lucky person when it comes to stuff like that."

Angus turned on the ignition, then thought for a minute and said, "You know what? I'm on a return trip. I don't gotta be anywhere till tomorrow, so I'll just make a little detour and drop you at home."

"You don't have to do that," Kit said, although she was already feeling relieved at the idea. The truth was that she *wasn't* looking forward to trying to find another safe ride in the middle of the night.

"It's no big deal," Angus said. "It's only about an hour out of the way if I take I-85. Only, you think you're rested up enough to keep me company? If I don't have somebody to talk to, I'm liable to get tired and need to pull off for a few winks."

"Yeah," Kit said. "I can do that for sure."

She wondered how far off the AT trail magic could occur. Even though Angus had never set foot on the trail, Kit absolutely considered him to be a trail angel, at least to her. He put the truck in gear and merged back onto the highway, and as they drove, she started telling him about all the different adventures she'd had on the trail. She had Angus laughing and smiling in no time, and Kit focused on the stories she'd made with Dodger and his crew because the ones involving Raven were just too painful to think about.

They arrived in Asheville around eight a.m. and Kit got to watch the sun rising in streaks of pink and orange over the mountains that had always been in her back yard. She saw them differently now, and she wasn't sure if the change was for the better or not.

When Angus pulled the big rig up in front of Kit's parents' house, he was careful not to engage the air brake in the cozy little suburban neighborhood. Most of the houses showed signs of life already, as people were getting ready to go to work and school and begin their days, and the little Cape Cod that Kit called home was no different. She could see a light on in the kitchen, where her parents were probably eating the same eggs and sausage that they had every day, drinking the same black coffee and reading the same Asheville Citizen-Times newspaper.

Kit sighed and Angus looked at her, then asked, "Something the matter?"

"No," she said. "It's just weird to be back in my life again. Thanks for the ride – I appreciate it more than you can know."

"My pleasure, little lady," he said. "Thanks for the company."

Kit grabbed her pack from the sleeper cabin where she'd stuffed it after she woke up in Richmond. Then she leaned impulsively over the center console to give Angus a hug. "Don't forget to send that postcard."

"I will if you send yours," he said.

"I don't know," Kit hedged. She glanced out the window and saw the front door opening, her mother coming onto the stoop in the same old pink robe that she'd been wearing for years. She waved, and Kit said, "There's my mom. I should go."

"You'll regret it if you have feelings for that fella and you don't try to make it work," Angus said. Kit nodded, then opened her door and hopped down from the truck.

"Thank you," she said again, then closed the door and Angus threw the truck into gear. She heard him pulling away down the street behind her as she walked up the sidewalk and her mom came running out to meet her.

"My baby," she said, throwing her arms around Kit's neck. "I missed you!"

"I missed you, too, Mom," she said, letting her pack fall to the grass as she hugged her.

"You were gone so long," her mom said. "I told your

father I thought we might have to send a rescue team to come get you."

"I just decided to stay longer," Kit said. "You knew where I was the whole time. I called you."

"I know," her mom said. "I just get scared when you do things so impulsively. I could never imagine that for my own life, so it's hard to picture my daughter being happy like that. Were you happy?"

"Yeah," Kit said. "I was. And then I wasn't anymore, so now I'm home."

"Honey, let her come inside the house before you grill her," Kit heard her dad say. She looked over her mom's shoulder and saw him standing in the doorway, already dressed for work in a dress shirt and tie.

"You're right," her mom said. "Are you hungry, baby? I'll fix you some eggs."

Kit's dad came and picked up her pack for her, and then Kit laughed, putting her hand to her forehead.

"What's wrong?" her mom asked.

Kit shook her head and said, "I bought trekking poles in Wind Gap right before I left the trail. I was always using Raven's and when I broke hers, she insisted that I get a pair of my own. And I just left them in the truck."

"Oh," her mom said, looking down the road in the direction that Angus had driven. "Maybe he'll come back."

"They're under the passenger seat. He won't find them for a while," Kit said, then chuckled again. "I am just not meant to own trekking poles. Oh well, maybe he can find some other hiker to gift them to – trail magic."

"What's that, dear?" her father asked.

Kit shook her head and said, "Oh, nothing. I'll explain it all later. Could I get those eggs? I actually am starving, come to think of it."

Her parents led her inside and they went into the kitchen. Her dad finished his breakfast while her mom cooked her a big plate of eggs with sausage patties the size of hockey pucks and the best cup of coffee she'd drank in two months. Kit wolfed it all down to the amusement of her parents, then looked at the time on the clock above the kitchen sink. It was nearly nine.

"Don't you have to go to work?" she asked.

"I'm going to take a personal day," her mom said, but Kit shook her head.

"Don't rearrange your lives on my account," she said. "I'm probably just going to take a long shower and then a nap. I barely got any sleep last night, and I'm thirty-four years old. You don't need to take care of me."

"I know, baby," her mom said. "It's just that I was worried about you. This whole trip was so spontaneous, I wasn't quite sure if your head was in the right place."

"It wasn't," Kit admitted. "But I think it is now, or if it's not, it will be soon. You guys don't have to worry about me. Go to work. Live your lives. I'll be here when you get home."

"Okay," her father said. "But don't sleep all day. Maybe you can call that temp agency of yours in the afternoon and see about getting a new job."

"I will," Kit promised. "Have I ever missed a rent payment before?"

She knew her parents worried about her, especially the way she played fast and loose with her work history. Her dad would much prefer it if she followed in his footsteps, finding a steady job where she could work for the rest of her life and then retire with a pension. But if she had that, she'd never have gone on the adventure she had.

Even though it ended badly, Kit could never regret the time she'd had with Raven.

"If I'm going to work, I really ought to get dressed," her mom said as if she'd just remembered she was still in her robe. She got up from the table after Kit reassured her that she'd be fine, then said, "Will you tell us all about your trip over dinner?"

"Of course," Kit said.

"And maybe about Raven, too?"

Kit frowned. "I'm not sure there's much to tell."

Her mom went down the hall to her bedroom to get changed, and her dad came over and kissed the top of Kit's head, wishing her a good day before he headed to work. Then Kit sat at the table alone, sipping hot, rich coffee and wondering what Raven's day was like. Had she left the motel yet, or was she still wallowing, too? Was she really going to enjoy being on the trail more without Kit there by her side?

Kit was sure that she wasn't going to enjoy going back to her old life without Raven, but she'd made a compelling argument against the two of them working out so there was nothing left to do but forget the whole thing.

KIT SPENT about an hour in the bath, with bubbles up to her chin and steam filling the bathroom. She washed all the dirt, sweat, and labor of the trail from her body, then crawled into bed and curled up in a pile of soft sheets and pillows.

It had been so long since she'd slept in her own bed, with the familiar smell of her mother's favorite detergent and the luxury of her own pillows. She'd slept on so many hard shelter platforms and spent so many nights with her hips hanging halfway over the edge of Raven's sleeping pad. It should have been the most wonderful relief to sleep in her own bed, but Kit couldn't close her eyes.

She couldn't turn her mind off.

The sun was streaming too brightly through her window, with nothing but a sheer curtain to filter it. The birds were chirping outside and the sounds of summer reminded her of everything she'd left behind in Pennsylvania.

Life was so much simpler on the Appalachian Trail, where all Kit needed to think about was putting one foot in front of the other and chasing after Raven. Back in Asheville, she had bills and relationships, the necessity of searching for a new job, and a phone full of voicemails that she couldn't bear to listen to.

It took a few hours to charge her phone after it had spent two months sitting neglected on her bedside table, but when it came back to life, Kit found over a dozen voicemails and even more text messages waiting for her.

A few were from her temp agency, and from friends who she hadn't bothered to tell when she set off for the trail, but most of them were from Sam.

Kit glanced through a couple of the texts and they were all in the same vein.

Call me back. We need to talk.

You left some stuff at my apartment. Let me know when you want to come get it.

I'm sorry things ended the way they did. It was bad timing.

I hope you're okay.

Kit spent several hours staring at the ceiling, trying to sleep and unable to close her eyes. Then she got up, erased everything on her phone, and called the temp agency.

"Hi, can I speak to Rachel?" she asked when an unfamiliar voice answered. The administrative assistants over there changed jobs about as often as Kit did, and this was nothing unexpected. What *did* come as a surprise, however, was the fact that Rachel didn't have anything for her.

"I'm sorry, Kit," she said. "I called you a few times last month after your Baker and Price gig ended, but you just dropped off the face of the earth. Where were you?"

"Hiking the Appalachian Trail," Kit said. "I'm back now, though, and I'm ready to work."

"I had to put your name on the bottom of the pile when you went incommunicado," Rachel said. "There's just nothing out there for you right now. Call me back in a couple of weeks if you still haven't found anything for yourself. Maybe we'll have an opening by then."

"There's nothing?" Kit asked. She'd been working for the same temp agency, and working with Rachel, for five years and there was *always* something. "Am I being punished for taking a vacation?"

"You didn't answer any of my calls for two months," Rachel said. "You're just going to have to wait your turn."

"Okay," Kit said.

She hung up the phone feeling discouraged, then spent the rest of the afternoon taking apart her hiking pack. She had no idea when would be the next time she'd have any use for a camping stove or her sleeping bag, so she cleaned it all and tucked it away in the back of her closet.

When her parents came home after work that night, her mom ordered a pizza and the three of them sat around the dining room table while Kit told them the best stories from her adventure. She told them about the meaning of trail magic and how freeing it had been to sleep under the stars and swim in a crystal-clear lake. Just like when she told Angus about her experience, she was careful to avoid too many mentions of Raven.

Unfortunately, her mom was not quite as subtle about her curiosity.

After the meal was over and Kit had spent the last hour talking in detail about all the different Appalachian Trail landmarks she'd seen, her mom abruptly said, "So, are you ever going to tell us about the girl you met?"

"What difference does it make?" Kit asked. "It's over now."

"It seemed like she meant a lot to you," her mom said. "Every time you called us from the trail, you had wonderful things to say about her. I could tell in your voice how much you cared about her."

"Must have been the fresh mountain air," Kit said flippantly, trying to brush off the comment.

"I don't know about that," her mom insisted. "I haven't heard you sound so in love in a long time. Probably since Monica."

"Mom, why do you have to bring that up?" Kit asked, getting testy.

"I just thought it was nice," she said. "Raven is obviously somebody special."

"Well, she thinks I'm immature and she'd rather hike alone," Kit said. "So it doesn't matter."

"I'm sorry, baby," her mom relented. "I didn't mean to upset you. I would like to hear about her one of these days, though. Coffee?"

Kit sighed and said, "Yes, please."

Her mom went into the kitchen to brew a pot, and Kit turned to her father. Now was a good time to change the conversation topic, so that when her mom came back there would be absolutely no danger of Raven or Monica coming up again. She said, "I called the temp agency this afternoon."

"Oh yeah?" her dad said. "Good. Are they going to be able to find you something?"

"Not for a while," Kit said. "They said there won't be

any openings for a couple of weeks, but don't worry about it. I'm not in the mood to wallow around the house all day so I'm going to go out tomorrow and find something to keep me busy."

"You know, I could probably get you an interview at my office," her dad said. This was an offer he'd made before, and Kit always turned it down – sometimes more gracefully than others. "They're hiring an office manager right now."

"I'm hardly qualified for a job like that," Kit said. "Thanks, Dad, but I think I'm going to find something on my own."

"I don't understand why you're so allergic to the idea of settling down and finding a good job," her dad said. *Here we go again.* Kit was suddenly not sure whether this topic was a trade up or down from talking about Raven. "You're a smart girl and I hate to see you throwing your life away like this."

"I'm not throwing anything away," Kit said. "I just don't want to get *stuck* somewhere."

"Is getting stuck really all that bad?" he asked. "What's wrong with stability?"

"It's fine until you start to rely on it," Kit said. "You just don't understand because you've never had it torn away from you."

Her dad put his hand on her shoulder and said, "It's been five years, Kit. I love you. Your mother loves you. We want what's best for you, but I'm starting to wonder if letting you live here is just another way for you to hide from reality. You *need* to get back out there.

Take a leap of faith. Trust the world enough to be a little vulnerable now and then. I promise you it's worth it."

Kit kept her eyes fixed on the polished wood surface of the dining table. It hurt her heart to hear those words, and it hurt even more to know that he was right, but she was powerless to act on it. Her last interaction with Raven was proof of that.

Her mother rejoined them, saying, "The coffee will be ready in about five minutes. I bought a strudel on my way home from the office."

Kit looked up and smiled at her, and then she told her dad, "My trail name was Parachute, you know."

THE NEXT MORNING, Kit woke up to an alarm clock for the first time in weeks. She put on a pair of black slacks and a suit jacket, combed her hair into a neat, professional ponytail, and printed off a couple copies of her resume. The two-month gap in employment didn't look great, but it was no worse than the dozen or so temp jobs she'd held over the last five years.

Kit called an Uber to take her into downtown Asheville, where there were strip malls aplenty. She was determined to walk from one end of the street to the other, stopping anywhere that had a Help Wanted sign in the window and leaving her resume. At first, it felt good to be outside. The sun was warm and her legs felt right at home trekking up the sidewalk. If she were still on the trail, she'd be making her way into New Jersey with Raven today.

After about an hour on the sidewalk, though, Kit's feet started to hurt and she could feel a blister forming on her heel. She'd worn a pair of dress flats to go with her suit, and suddenly she was missing her trail boots terribly.

She was nearly to the end of the row of strip malls before she finally went into the right store. It was a sandwich shop and Kit was a little overdressed in her suit jacket and dress shoes, but she plucked the sign from the window and set it down on the counter, asking, "Can I please apply for this job?"

The teenager in a hairnet behind the counter shouted over his shoulder to get his boss's attention, and it turned out that was all Kit needed to do to land her next job. A short interview and a brief tour around the shop later, and she had an apron and orders to report to work for her first shift the next day.

It wasn't the job of her dreams, and as she went back outside with the apron thrown over her shoulder, Kit decided to walk home. It was more than an hour back to the suburbs on foot, but Kit had nothing better to do for the rest of the day and everything was within walking distance if she wanted it to be.

21

RAVEN

Raven felt more alone than ever when she hitchhiked back to the trail the next morning.

Even before she met Kit, when she was Lone Wolf and she did everything by herself, she didn't feel so isolated as she did now. She slept in the big motel bed all alone – or tried to – and ate breakfast at a little diner in town. She walked all day in utter silence, nothing but the sound of the earth crunching under her boots and the songs of birds overhead to keep her company.

She thought a lot about Kit and the fight that they'd had. Raven wished there were other things to think about, but unless she wanted to use her phone to listen to music and drain the battery prematurely, there was nothing else to keep her mind occupied.

She'd said a lot of things in anger and frustration last night, and it wasn't really Kit's fault. They'd been mutually pushing each other away in a fierce, last-ditch effort at self-preservation, and Kit running away was simply the logical conclusion.

Still, Raven wished she was here.

She wished she wasn't so stubborn and so insistent on her own solitude.

She was alone at the shelter that night, too. If ever she needed the boisterous company of Dodger and his crew to keep her occupied, this was the night. But as she set up her camp stove in the middle of a deserted campsite, Raven thought it was probably appropriate that she should feel this alone.

She made a packet of chicken-flavored rice and when it was ready, she realized that she'd gotten so sick of it over the last 1,300 miles that she couldn't bear to take a bite. So instead of eating it, Raven just stared at it sullenly for about an hour. It congealed into a solid mass in the bottom of her pot and then she committed a cardinal thru-hiking sin – she dug a hole on the outskirts of the campsite and buried her food.

She crawled into her tent well before dark, curling up into a little ball on the sleeping pad that suddenly felt unnecessarily large without Kit beside her. She fell asleep counting the miles to Katahdin and praying that they went quickly.

She was also praying she hadn't made a horrible mistake in Wind Gap.

What adventure was there without Kit?

RAVEN'S STEPS became more mechanical with every day.

She passed fellow thru-hikers, both northbound and southbound, and she stayed in shelters both empty and full. She ate when her stomach told her to, and rested when her legs said she needed to. She lived and died by her itinerary because there was nothing left to do.

If she let herself think about it too hard, she would realize that there was no point to any of this if she was just going to reduce the journey to a trip of 2,190 lonely miles. But she was in New Jersey now, with just seven more states between her and Mount Katahdin. It would be equally futile to stop or to keep going.

Raven had her worst day about a week after Kit left her in Wind Gap. She'd slogged her way through the New Jersey stretch of the trail and crossed over into New York the previous day. She was on Bear Mountain and it was a rainy, dreary day.

The rain was cold and it plastered Raven's clothes against her. She was uncomfortable with it all over again, trying in vain to keep her shirt from sticking to her chest. She just wanted to be warm and dry, somewhere with decent food and a soft bed.

Instead, she was all alone on a rocky part of the trail that Kit would have absolutely adored.

It was called the Lemon Squeezer, and it reminded Raven of the Rock Maze, where no matter how much nagging she did, Kit refused to be careful or go slow. She'd taken so much joy in scrambling over those boulders, like a kid on a playground, and her excitement had been contagious.

Here, there were enormous boulders and glacial rocks to navigate, only these ones were so large there was no climbing over or walking around. All hikers could do was squeeze right through the narrow spaces in between rocks the size of houses. The rain slid down the sides of them, making them slick and cold, and Raven shivered as she trudged onward.

She hadn't seen Dodger, Break Time and Eagle Scout since Damascus, and she knew she'd never see Kit again. She ran into a few other hikers that she knew now and again, but she didn't bond with a single one of them the way she had connected with Kit.

As she was sliding through a particularly tight space, Raven's pack got caught behind her and she tried to push onward. She leaned forward, her pack sliding against the wet rock and wedging it even tighter. She tried to go back, but her pack wouldn't budge.

Forward.

Backward.

She couldn't make any progress more than an inch in any direction.

And that's when she lost it.

Raven started crying and then sobbing. Her tears mixed with the rain and she smacked her shoulders against the filthy, rough rocks on either side of her. She was trapped and alone, and the journey that was supposed to free her had become a nightmare.

She looked up at the sky and screamed, her voice

carrying across the rocks in an echo. Then she slumped down, sliding out of her pack and sitting on the muddy ground, her pack still wedged in the rocks about a foot above her. She put her head in her hands and cried, wondering how in the hell she'd ended up here.

Then after a while, she ran out of tears and wiped her face with the front of her shirt. It was damp from the rain, but at least she could keep the stiff salt water of her tears from drying on her cheeks. She took a few deep breaths and stood up.

She knew exactly how she got here.

One step at a time, one foot in front of the other.

And that was how she'd get to Katahdin, too, because she had no choice.

She wiggled her pack until she was able to get it free from the rocks, then she turned it sideways and continued onward, holding it in front of her as she made her way out of the Lemon Squeezer.

She was shivering and wet by the time she came to the next shelter, and even though her itinerary called for her to keep hiking for another few miles to the next campsite that day, Raven threw her pack down on the wet ground and called it a day. She took off her wet shirt and wrung it out as best she could, then erected her tent and climbed inside.

The rain continued to patter on the nylon sides, and it was much too early to do anything other than shiver and wait to become hungry enough to bother with dinner.

Raven took out her phone after a few minutes. She

checked the battery. There was more than fifty percent charge left, and she'd be stopping in Pawling in two days to pick up her next drop box. She could afford to play some music if she wanted to, but sitting in a tent all alone with the rain and wind beating on the sides of her tent, she wasn't sure there was any music that would soothe her.

She started to think about all the things her sister had been so worried about at the beginning of her journey. Annabel was convinced that Raven would be eaten by bears, or attacked by predators just lurking in the woods and looking for their next hiker victim.

I bet you never thought I'd be my own worst enemy, Raven thought with a smirk.

She had a sudden impulse to call her sister and tell her this hysterical joke. It was about three in the afternoon in New York, so it would be about noon in Seattle. Maybe she could catch Anna on her lunch break.

Raven crossed her fingers and tried to make the call.

She had one bar, and not a whole lot of hope considering there were so many enormous boulders nearby that would make fantastic signal blockers. But she hated the idea of spending the entire afternoon alone in a tent that was rapidly getting humid from the rain. She was miserable, and she just wanted to talk to her sister.

"Hello?"

"Anna!" Raven exclaimed as soon as the call connected.

"Raven?"

"Yeah! Can you hear me?" she asked. The connection was filled with static, but it was so good to hear Annabel's voice.

"Yes. Where are you?" Anna asked.

"I'm in New York," Raven said. "I just needed to talk to someone familiar."

"Is everything okay?" Annabel asked. "Aren't you hiking with that girl, Kit?"

"Not anymore," Raven said. "We went our separate ways last week."

That seemed to be the most diplomatic way she could find of describing it, and Annabel seemed to accept that explanation. Raven was grateful, until she asked, "How come?"

"I don't even know anymore," she said, breaking down for the second time that day. She didn't cry this time, though. She didn't have the energy required. She sighed and said, "We got into a big fight. I said some things I regret, and she went home. I've spent the past week thinking that I've got her parents' number stored in my phone because I let her borrow it to call them. All I want to do is call her and make sure she's okay, and tell her I'm sorry, but I can't."

"Why not?" Annabel asked. "If that's what you want, then maybe that's what she wants, too. Maybe she's sitting by the phone, waiting for you to call her."

"I don't think so," Raven said. "And even if she was, it's not a good idea. We're too afraid of getting hurt by each other."

"I'm sorry, big sis, but that's one of the most ridiculous things I've ever heard," Annabel said.

"I know," Raven answered. "But the damage is done. She's in North Carolina and I'm in New York. It's over. Look, I called because I needed to hear a familiar voice, so please tell me about what's going on in your life. Tell me about the normal world and what's going on beyond the trail."

"Okay," Annabel said. "Well, I'm up for a promotion - just found out this morning. And I've got a date this weekend."

"The guy from the coffee shop you told me about last time?" Raven asked. Annabel confirmed, and Raven said, "That's great. Tell me more."

She cradled the phone to her ear, trying to find the clearest reception she could inside her tiny tent, and she talked to Annabel for the next thirty minutes before she finally felt pragmatism beginning to gnaw at her again.

"I should probably go," she said when there was a lull in the conversation. "I have to reserve enough battery to last me another forty-eight hours. If you talk to Mom and Dad before I do, tell them I'll call them from Pawling in a couple days."

"Okay," Annabel said. "But I'm not telling them you broke up with your trail girlfriend. They're going to be devastated."

Raven rolled her eyes. Leave it to her sister to make her feel worse about Kit, all the way from the opposite coast. She said, "I know. They really liked her. They even started putting extra treats in my drop boxes for her. I'll have to tell them to stop so I don't have to carry around the extra weight."

"Are you doing okay out there?" Annabel asked, detecting the shift in Raven's mood back to sullenness.

"I've got no choice," Raven said. "Like everything else, I just have to walk it off."

"Well, you're in the home stretch," Annabel said, trying to be comforting. Raven just snorted.

"I have five hundred miles left," she pointed out. "I don't think that can be considered a home stretch by any measure."

"It's more than three quarters of the way there, though," Annabel said. "That has to count for something."

"I'll be honest," Raven said. "I'm not sure what."

"I'll tell you one thing," Annabel said. "When I fly out to Maine to meet you with Mom and Dad, I'm going to be impressed as hell. I mean, I already am, but I'll be even *more* proud of you when I see you coming down off that mountain with your head held high. You know you're my role model, right?"

Raven laughed again and said, "Oh, shut up. I am not."

"You are," Annabel said. "I know it sounds corny and kind of weird because we don't usually talk like that. But it's true. I'd be lucky to be half the woman you are."

"Thank you," Raven said grudgingly. She wasn't used to taking compliments, and she wasn't sure quite what to say, so she just settled for honesty. "I needed to hear that."

"I know," Annabel said. "Now get back out there and kick that mountain's butt."

22

KIT

It was a slow afternoon at Crusts Off Sandwiches.

Kit had been there two weeks and it already felt like a hundred. She'd spent a single day being trained on everything from the menu to the cash register and the bread ovens, and then she was left to her own devices. With nothing but a hairnet, a green apron, and a pimply teen working his first summer job to keep her company, Kit's mind wandered.

She'd given up waiting for Rachel at the temp agency to call her back, and that was okay because Kit wasn't sure she could handle another desk job in a cubicle farm – not now, anyway. Even after two weeks, her mind was still on the Appalachian Trail. She missed having nothing to worry about except the day's hike, and the various ways she could find to entertain and seduce Raven along the way. Kit loved making her laugh, making her face light up, making her serious façade fall away to reveal the real Raven underneath.

Now she had nothing to think about all day long while she stood behind the counter of Crusts Off except the fact that she'd screwed all that up when she got scared about how much she was feeling for Raven.

She kept busy by pacing back and forth behind the counter like a lion at the zoo. It wasn't the Appalachian Trail, but at least she could move her body and she wasn't chained to a desk chair. Sometimes, like during the daily lunch rush, when people from the various businesses in the area all flooded into the shop, she had a reason to pace.

Most of the time, it was just annoying to her coworkers. Jason, the kid who had been standing at the counter when Kit first walked into the shop and asked for a job, found it particularly irritating.

"Seriously, stand still," he said dispassionately to her this afternoon, on her hundredth trip up and down the length of the counter. "Why are you so keyed up, anyway?"

"I hiked thirteen hundred miles in the last two months," Kit said. "It's a habit."

"Well, break it," he said. "You're making me nervous."

"I'm sorry," Kit said. She put her hands on the edge of the counter to hold herself in place.

"Thank you," Jason answered.

Kit had worked with him a lot over the past couple of weeks, and he was content to just stand with his feet glued to the floor from the start of their shift until the end unless a customer came in. Then he'd reluctantly reach for a pair of disposable gloves and slowly assemble their sandwich.

"Don't you get bored standing in the same spot all day?" she asked.

"No," Jason said. "I'm saving my energy for later."

"Like you've got a limited supply?" Kit quipped. "You're seventeen."

"Yeah, and I got stuff to do at night," he said. "Parties to go to. Girls to meet."

Kit pretended to understand, but most of the time when Jason talked about his life outside the sandwich shop, she was wondering when she'd gotten so old. It seemed like just yesterday, Kit had been in high school, working a summer job to make money so she could have fun with her friends and have no cares in the world.

Now, Jason's life seemed as alien to her as her life was to him.

He probably thought that she was a total loser, still living with her parents, single, and just starting a new job at the ripe old age of thirty-four. If he did, he was at least kind enough not to mention it out loud.

Kit squeezed the edge of the counter in her hands, resisting the urge to start pacing again, and Jason just shut off his brain and stood there with his arms crossed over his chest. She used to be able to do things like that. Now, she spent her time tidying up the counter and cutting tomatoes in advance of the dinner rush.

The restaurant was nearly empty at the moment, lunch having ended for most people several hours ago. There were just a couple of retired men in a booth toward the back of the dining room, picking at sandwiches and playing a leisurely game of chess with a board they'd brought with them.

She'd just released her grip on the counter and reached for a head of lettuce to shred when the chime above the door sounded. Kit set down the lettuce and looked up as her next customer approached the counter.

"Sam," she said.

Her ex-girlfriend stood on the other side of the counter, looking just as surprised as Kit felt.

"You work here?" Sam asked.

"Umm, yeah," Kit answered. "For about two weeks."

"I've been calling you," Sam said, an edge rising into her voice. "You ghosted me."

"Busted," Jason said, and Kit shot him a glare.

"We're almost out of gloves," she said. "Can you get a new box out of the supply closet?"

He rolled his eyes and went down the length of the counter, then disappeared into the back room. Kit turned her attention back to Sam.

"What can I get started for you?" she asked, surprising herself.

"Really?" Sam asked. "You're not even going to acknowledge me?"

"I just don't know what to say," Kit answered. "I'm sorry I didn't return any of your calls. I went on a trip."

"Without your phone?"

"Yes, actually," Kit said. "Anyway, *you're* the one who broke up with *me*, remember?"

"Yes, I do," Sam said. "But I figured you'd at least

want your things back. You just disappeared and I was worried about you."

"I'm sorry that I worried you," Kit said. "I just had to get away for a while and I didn't really expect you to call."

"So where did you go?" Sam asked.

"To the mountains," Kit said. "I hiked the Appalachian Trail for two months."

Sam's eyes went wide. "Really?"

"Yeah," Kit said. "And now I'm back home, I'm making sandwiches, and that's it. Look, did you come in here on your lunch break or what?"

Sam was wearing a tailored suit jacket and an A-line skirt. Every strand of her hair was tucked neatly into place and she always had been the consummate professional. Kit knew her office was around this area somewhere, but she hadn't expected to run into Sam, especially because she'd always been so meticulous about packing her lunch when they were dating.

"Yeah," Sam said. "I come in here every once in a while if I forget to pack a lunch. It's the healthiest thing within walking distance of my office."

"Let me make you a sandwich, then," Kit said. "What'll it be?"

"Can we talk for a minute while I eat?" Sam asked. "I'm worried about you."

"We're not together anymore," Kit pointed out. "That's not your job anymore."

"It's no one's *job* to worry about you, Kit," Sam said.

"People do that when they care about you. I'll have the turkey club."

Kit made Sam's sandwich, then she called Jason back from the stock closet and asked him to watch the counter. He gave her a snarky reply about having it all under control, and then Kit went with Sam over to one of the booths and slid in across from her.

"You don't need to worry about me," she said while Sam took a bite of her sandwich. "I'm fine. How about you?"

"I'm good," Sam said. She glanced down at the countertop, then said, "You should know I'm dating someone."

"Good for you," Kit said. "Anyone I know?"

"My friend Jessica?" Sam said. "You met her once or twice."

"Yeah, I liked her," Kit said. "For the record, I didn't think you were stalking me at my sandwich shop gig because you secretly wanted to get back together."

"You know I didn't say any of those hurtful things to you on the day that we broke up because I wanted to hurt you," Sam said abruptly. "I said them because I was hoping they would wake you up and show you that you have so much more potential than what you're living up to. Kit, why are you here?"

"The temp agency didn't have anything for me," she said.

"You can do better than the temp agency, too," Sam said. "You could have a career, and a girlfriend, and a life. Why do you push everyone away so hard?"

"Because it's uncomfortable to be close to people," Kit said. "I met someone since the last time we saw each other, too, except she rejected me. She didn't want me anymore and it really hurt. Who can live with that?"

"We all have to," Sam said. "It's a part of life. Don't run from your life, Kit."

"Everyone thinks they know me better than I know myself," Kit said with a sigh. "Maybe I know what I can handle."

"And maybe you don't give yourself enough credit," Sam said. She looked at the watch on her wrist and started wrapping up her sandwich. "I'm sorry, I've got a meeting in fifteen minutes. I have to go."

Kit stood up and looked toward the counter. Jason was watching the two of them, not even trying to hide the fact that he was eavesdropping because he had nothing better to do. She turned back to Sam, who slid out of the booth and held out her hand.

Kit took it, and Sam said, "It was good to see you. I'm glad you're doing okay."

"You, too," Kit said. "Good luck with Jessica."

"Good luck to you, too," Sam said.

She left, and Kit went back behind the counter, ignoring the look that Jason was giving her, like he was waiting for some juicy gossip to entertain him for the rest of the afternoon. Kit put her hands on the counter and stood in place, thinking about what Sam had said.

When her shift ended that afternoon and her manager showed up to relieve her and Jason, Kit took off her green apron and handed it to him.

"I'm really sorry," she said. "But this isn't where I'm supposed to be right now."

23

RAVEN

Raven soldiered on.

She felt a little better after talking to her sister, and when she stopped in Pawling to pick up another drop box and called her parents, they tried their best to lift her spirits as well. Raven sat on a bench outside the post office and opened her drop box, which her mother had opened and stuffed with all sorts of taffy, candy, and sweets for her to share with Kit, and she had to tell them the truth.

"Kit and I split up," she said with the phone tucked into the crook of her neck as she packed her fresh supply of food into her bag. "You can stop sending me extra treats now."

"Annabel told us," her mom said sadly. "I already shipped the next two boxes. Maybe you can find another hiker friend to share the extra stuff with."

"I'll have to," Raven said. "It's too heavy to carry on my own."

"I'm sorry, honey," her mom said. "What happened? I thought you two were getting along."

"We were," Raven said. "I really liked her, but it just wasn't right. I guess you can't *really* expect to find your soulmate in the middle of the wilderness by chance."

"Chance is all we have," her father cut in, surprising Raven because he spoke so sparingly. She wasn't even sure he was still on the line most of the time when she called until they said their goodbyes. "No one meets the significant people in their lives on purpose."

"I guess that's true," Raven said.

"Well, if it's meant to be, then you'll find her again," her mother said.

"No," Raven answered. "She went home. I won't be seeing her again."

"Just keep your chin up and your eye on the prize, then," her mom said. "You're almost there and we're all so proud of you, sweetie."

"Thank you," Raven said. Then she hung up and spent an hour or two charging her phone while she ate a few of the candy bars her parents had sent for Kit. She passed a couple southbound hikers on her way back to the trail and handed off the rest of her excess to them.

The trail was lonely for the next few weeks, and by the time Raven entered New Hampshire – the last state before Maine and the northern terminus – she'd given up all hope of running into people she knew. There were more and more southbound hikers at the shelters at night, bright-eyed and just beginning their adventures, and Raven had reverted back into the comfortable, solitary Lone Wolf persona that she'd begun her adventure with.

She'd had a lot of weeks to learn to be okay with that, and she was starting to think that it was quite fitting. She began the trail alone and she'd finish it alone.

Then one day, around mile 1,800, a familiar set of faces appeared on the edge of Raven's shelter.

"Dodger?" she asked as the three Merry Men approached the campsite. "Is that you?"

"Who else would it be?" he asked, as chipper and boyish as ever. He came right up to Raven and threw down his pack, giving her an unexpected hug as Eagle Scout and Break Time brought up the rear of their caravan and joined them.

Raven stepped back and said, "I thought I'd lost you guys, or that you threw in the towel."

"Never!" Dodger shouted into the trees, his hands on his hips in a conquering pose.

"We've done a lot of yellow blazing and taken a lot of zero days off-trail," Eagle Scout said. "But we're bound and determined to get to Katahdin."

"Speak for yourselves," Break Time said. "I could have stopped back in Tennessee and I'd be just as happy with my trip."

Raven smiled and asked, "How much of the trail would you say that you've actually hiked?"

"Oh, at least a couple hundred miles," Eagle Scout said sarcastically.

They all laughed, and then Dodger looked around

the campsite. He saw Raven's one-person tent, and her lonely pack laying on the dirt beside it, and he frowned. "Where's Parachute?"

"North Carolina," Raven said.

"She went home?" Dodger asked, his expression marked with mild horror at the idea.

"Yeah," Raven said. "We split up in Pennsylvania."

"Shit," Dodger said. He looked around at the empty campsite, probably imagining how awful it would be to spend a night all alone as Raven had been doing for the last three hundred miles. Then, because there was nothing else to say, he smirked and said, "She proved you right."

"What do you mean?" Raven asked.

"You didn't think she could make it all the way to the end," he said. "Damn. You really *are* a Lone Wolf."

Raven squirmed a bit at this blunt assessment, and when Eagle Scout caught it he offered, "You could hike with us for a while. I can't promise we won't end up taking a day or two off when we get to Woodstock, but if you can tolerate our speed, you're welcome to join us."

"I appreciate it," Raven said. "But at this point, I'd really like to just get to Maine already. Would you guys eat dinner with me, though? It sure is nice to see some familiar faces."

"Of course," Break Time said, then laughed and added, "What choice do we have?"

Dodger smacked his arm, and then the three of them sat down next to Raven and they all got out their camp stoves to cook up their dinners. While they ate, Eagle Scout gave Raven an overview of their trip, and ended the account by saying with a roll of his eyes, "These two are going to spend the next year and a half bragging about how they hiked the Appalachian Trail, and I'm not going to tell *anyone* I did it for fear of embarrassment at how very little we actually hiked."

THE NEXT MORNING, Raven got up with the dawn and started to dismantle her tent. The soft sounds of nylon being folded and put away stirred Dodger out of sleep and he crawled off the shelter platform to join her.

"So how does it feel to have *actually* hiked almost two thousand miles?" Dodger asked.

Raven considered it for a moment, wanting to give him a real answer, but it was unquantifiable, so she just said, "Not quite as life-changing as I hoped."

"Don't tell me you're *still* expecting to find yourself up here," Dodger said. "You know better than that, Lone Wolf. The trail doesn't have the power to transform."

Kit had been telling Raven that all along, and yet somehow when Dodger said it, his words sounded so much harsher than hers ever had. He didn't know Raven's struggle or the demons she'd brought with her onto the trail, so how could he guess what was running beneath the surface of her mind so easily?

"Everybody comes out here thinking they're going to

wake up on the side of a mountain one day, breathe in some fresh mountain air and shed their old identity like a snakeskin," he went on. "I get it. I thought that too at first, but it's nonsense."

"Is it really too much to ask after spending six months of my life out here?" Raven asked. She was getting frustrated with him, and with his determination not to let her keep living with that idea. She was all alone out here and she needed it to keep her company.

She needed to believe there was something waiting for her on the summit of Katahdin.

"Too much to ask of 2,190 miles of primitive trails, outdoor toilets, and body odor?" Dodger asked with a smirk. "Yeah, I think it's too much. Especially if you're going to stubbornly hold onto that stupid Lone Wolf thing you've been doing since day one."

Raven scowled at him, then shoved her tent into her pack and zipped it up. "I have to get going. There are still a lot of miles to cover."

"Okay," Dodger said. "Just do yourself a favor and lower your expectations for Katahdin. There's no secret waiting for you on top of that mountain."

"Thanks," Raven said grudgingly. "I hope I'll see you guys around. Good luck if not."

"Good luck to you, too," Dodger answered. Then he went back to the shelter to retrieve his camp stove and cook breakfast, and Raven set out for another solitary day on the trail.

RAVEN WASN'T surprised when she lost track of the guys again. They weren't at the shelter where she stopped that night, and she missed them when she went into Woodstock for her next drop box.

So she settled back into her routine, hiking alone and keeping herself entertained. She found peaceful places to meditate along the trail and swam a few more times in the lakes along the way – fully clothed, of course, because she didn't have the confidence to skinny dip without Kit by her side, urging her on. She listened to music on her phone when the silence became too great, and she called her parents and Annabel at each trail town she stopped at over the next couple of weeks.

Then on her hundred and thirtieth day on the trail, Raven hiked into Monson, Maine.

She was ten days away from Mount Katahdin and the end of the Appalachian Trail, but this would be her very last trail town. After Monson, she'd enter what was known as the Hundred Mile Wilderness, a week-long hike through isolated forests that would take her right up to Baxter State Park and the northern terminus.

Once she was out of the wilderness, there was just a single day more before she'd reach the base of Katahdin, and one more day to the summit and the big wooden sign marking the northern end of the Appalachian Trail.

When Raven arrived in Monson, she felt a sudden urge to stay there. She had no plans to get a motel room or to take a day off from hiking, but the idea of taking those first steps into the Hundred Mile Wilderness scared her.

She was so close to the end, and Dodger was right – she had unrealistic expectations about what she was going to find there. If she just stayed in Monson, then she couldn't be disappointed when her adventure came to an end.

What if there was no sense of accomplishment?

What if she was just the same old Raven, scared and insecure?

What if she went back to Chicago and everything was the *same?*

With fluttering pulse, she went to the post office and picked up her drop box, then followed the same routine that she'd been sticking to ever since the beginning of the trail. She found a place to sit down and charge her phone, and while she was transferring the contents of her drop box into her pack, she called her parents. Today, they had to finalize their plans to come pick her up at the end of the trail.

"I should be finished on August 16th," Raven said. She'd planned every other part of her journey down to the mile, so really, there was no *should* about it. She *would* leave Monson in a few hours, she *would* spend the next six days in the Hundred Mile Wilderness, and she *would* reach the end of her journey on the sixteenth.

As long as she didn't let her nerves get the best of her.

"And we're going to meet you at the state park that evening," her mother filled in. "I've got our motel reservations in Millinocket all ready, and the next day we'll pick your sister up at the airport in Bangor. Then we road trip back to Chicago."

"Sounds good, Mom," Raven said. "I really appreciate you guys taking your vacation time from work to come out here and pick me up."

"Honey, I've missed you so much," her mom said. "I can't *wait* to spend my vacation time catching up with you. And you better have a ton of photos and stories to tell me about your trip while we drive back."

"Don't worry," Raven said with a smile. She glanced up the road as a blonde girl in a tie-dyed shirt and hiking boots was coming up the road toward her. Raven stared at the girl for a second, startled by her resemblance to Kit. Impossible. Then she turned her attention back to her mom and said, "I've got more than enough stories to keep us occupied."

"How excited are you to be nearly done?" her mom asked. "It must feel like such an accomplishment."

"It is..." Raven said, although she trailed off in the middle of her sentence. Out of the corner of her eye, she could see that the blonde was making a beeline for her, and the closer she got, the more she looked like Kit.

No way.

"Raven." The girl said her name from a few yards away and it made Raven's legs feel weak. She turned to look at her again and her eyes were not deceiving her. It really was Kit.

"Mom, I have to call you back," Raven said, dropping the phone on her pack and running down the road to meet Kit.

Kit threw her arms open and caught Raven in a fierce

embrace. Any lingering doubts that this had been a mirage brought on by the intense solitude of hiking alone for the last couple of months finally faded as Raven felt Kit's arms around her, and she started to cry against Kit's neck.

24

KIT

"What are you doing here?" Raven asked. Her voice sounded watery and it made a lump form in Kit's throat, too.

She had no idea what to expect when she finally found Raven. She'd been lingering in Monson for two days, waiting for Raven to arrive, and she had been worrying the whole time. What if Raven didn't want to see her? What if she showed up with some other hiker and Kit saw that she was replaceable? What if she did her calculations wrong and missed Raven entirely, and then they never saw each other again?

What if she never had a chance to apologize?

"I had to tell you that I'm sorry," Kit said. She didn't want to let go of Raven for fear she'd slip away again. "I shouldn't have left, and I shouldn't have put so much energy into keeping you at arm's length. I was afraid of how much I was feeling for you."

"I'm sorry, too," Raven said. Her arms were tight

around Kit and that was comforting. "I pushed you away and you just reacted accordingly."

Kit finally pulled away and wiped some dampness from Raven's cheeks, then laughed and said, "We're both screwed up. Do you think we can work on that together?"

"I hope so," Raven said. "I'm so happy to see you."

"I'm happy to see you, too," Kit said. "I thought I ruined everything when I walked out of that motel room in Wind Gap."

Raven breathed deeply, then said, "I thought the same thing. How did you find me?"

"Your ridiculously specific itinerary," Kit said with a laugh. "I knew you'd have a drop box waiting for you before the Hundred Mile Wilderness, and I just had to do some calculations about how fast you were hiking to guess when you'd get here. I was off by two days, but I found out that diner across the street serves excellent blueberry pie while I was waiting."

Raven laughed and threw her arms around Kit again, then whispered in her ear, "I'm glad you came back."

"Not only that," Kit said, "but I took the time to do some proper packing before I came. I've got trekking poles, a sleeping pad of my own, and I've been practicing setting up my tent just in case you were willing to let me finish up the trail with you."

Raven smiled and said, "I don't want to finish it *without* you."

They kissed and all of Kit's fears melted away. She felt at home again for the first time since she left the trail, and she decided at that moment that she'd do whatever it took to stay by Raven's side. It was where she belonged.

"Oh, shit," Raven said. "I have to call my parents back. I sort of hung up on them when I saw you."

Kit sat down on the bench and waited while Raven finished transferring the contents of her drop box into her pack and called her parents back. She put the phone on speaker and Kit said hello to them. She felt nervous, wondering what Raven had told them about her in the time since she left and what they would think about her, but they were nice and they sounded happy that the two of them had been reunited.

Raven finished her conversation with her mother, and then when she hung up, Kit circled her arms around Raven's waist and pulled her into her lap to kiss her again.

"I missed you so much," she said.

"I missed you, too," Raven answered. "You have no idea how much."

"Should we go get some pie?" Kit suggested. "I'll tell you how much I missed you, and you can tell me everything *I* missed on the trail."

"Sounds like a plan," Raven said.

They walked hand-in-hand across the street to the only restaurant on the main drag of town. The hostess said hi to Kit when they walked in, and Kit explained to Raven that she'd eaten there five times in the last two days while she was waiting, not wanting to deplete the stock she'd brought with her for the final leg of the hike.

Then they sat down in a booth at the front of the restaurant and Kit let her foot rest against Raven's beneath the table. She didn't want to be apart from her - even a table's length was too far. They ordered grilled cheese sandwiches on Kit's recommendation, and then Raven took Kit's hand.

"I'm sorry for what I said in Wind Gap," she said. "It had a lot more to do with my own insecurities than it had to do with you, and it wasn't fair. I had a lot of issues to work through, and I honestly still do, but if you can look past them, I want to be with you – now *and* when we get off the trail."

"I don't have to look past *anything*," Kit said. "I think you're amazing exactly as you are, and that's all I ever wanted to hear – that you're willing to try. I think we could both use a little practice opening up to other people, and I've never actually *wanted* to do that with anyone except you. You make me want to be a better person, Raven."

Raven squeezed her hand and said, "So do you. You've *already* made me a better person."

"So let's hike to Katahdin together?" Kit asked. "And then see what life holds for us on the other side?"

"Yes," Raven said, nodding her head emphatically, making Kit break into a broad grin. "I mean, there are a lot of questions to answer. Where will we live? How will our parents feel-"

"Stop," Kit said with a laugh. "We will figure out the answers to all those questions, but we don't have to know them *right this minute*. We've got all the time in the world and it's okay to jump without a parachute sometimes."

Raven smiled, and then the waitress came back to the table with a couple plates for them. While they ate, Raven took out her phone and showed Kit all the photos she'd taken between Pennsylvania and Maine, and told her about the best sights she'd seen along the way. Then Kit told Raven about her brief stint as a sandwich artist, and how nothing in the real world felt real without Raven by her side.

25

RAVEN

When they were finished eating – and after they'd each demolished one of the best slices of blueberry pie Raven had ever eaten, she followed Kit down the street to a motel where she'd been staying.

"I just need to get my pack and check out," Kit said as she unlocked the door and Raven stayed on the sidewalk outside. "Are you sure you don't want to come in?"

She was smiling at Raven, with a look that left no room for interpretation. Raven glanced inside the room and saw a king-sized bed that dominated the space. The temptation was strong, but she stood her ground and gave Kit a wink.

"If I set foot in that room, we're never going to make it to Katahdin," Raven said. "My parents are going to be waiting for me on the sixteenth."

"Damn your itinerary," Kit said with a grin. Then she went inside and gathered her things while Raven stood outside the door and looked down the street to the wilderness that awaited them. There would be plenty of time for motel rooms and reunions *after* Katahdin.

"You know," Raven said through the doorway, "I had a really hard time sitting across from you in that diner. Every single second, all I wanted to do was sweep everything off the table and leap across it to get to you."

"Why didn't you?" Kit asked as she came back to the door with her pack on her back and her new trekking poles in hand.

"Those aren't the poles you bought in Wind Gap," Raven said, puzzled.

"It's a long story," Kit said. Then she grabbed Raven by the front of her shirt and pulled her into the room, pressing her up against the wall beside the door and kissing her hard. Their bodies pressed together and Raven could feel Kit's hips against her own, seeking her.

Raven put her hands on Kit's waist, squeezing her, and slid her tongue across Kit's lips. She let out a groan and then pushed Kit gently back, breaking the connection between them. Raven let out a tortured sigh and said, "We have to get back on that trail immediately, before I lose control."

"Wouldn't want that," Kit teased.

"Please," Raven said. "Don't make me call my family and tell them I'm not going to be able to meet them on time because I'm trapped in a motel room with a siren. I'm too old for that kind of embarrassment."

Kit laughed and stepped away. She smiled angelically and said, "Okay. Let's get hiking, then, because the sooner we get to the shelter tonight, the sooner I can tear your clothes off."

They stepped outside and Kit locked the door, then they went to the motel office so she could return her key and check out. Then they got back on the trail. Kit chattered eagerly about what it would be like to reach Mount Katahdin, and they talked about all the different possibilities for what their life would look like when they finished this adventure.

Raven had her job waiting for her in Chicago and she'd need to be ready to teach the fall semester almost immediately when she got home, but Kit was jobless once again and ready for another adventure in a new city. It made the most sense that she'd come to Illinois with Raven and figure something out there – maybe even get a *real* job, something that didn't have an expiration date attached to it.

When they arrived at the campsite that night, Raven pulled Kit into her arms and asked, "Are we really doing this? It's not just a fantasy?"

"Not to me," Kit said. "I'll go on any adventure as long as you want to bring me with you."

"Good," Raven said. "I will, too."

Then Kit smiled and pulled out of the embrace, saying, "Watch this. We're going to sleep in *my* tent tonight."

Raven grinned and watched Kit deftly assemble her tent, then Kit pulled her inside on the pretense of taking a tour.

They lay down on her sleeping pad and Kit circled

Raven in her arms, holding her close in a protective embrace. They kissed, and then made love. The first time was frantic, satisfying a craving that they'd both been powerless to act on for the last few months. The second time was slower, appreciating every inch of each other's bodies and the fact that they were together, two souls who had found each other in the middle of the wilderness and belonged to each other.

THE WEEK that Raven and Kit passed through the Hundred Mile Wilderness went faster than any other part of the trail. During the day, they let their imaginations go wild with possibilities for their life together – apartments and careers, vacation adventures and family. At night, they found as much solitude as they could, either at shelters where they were lucky enough to be alone, or by camping illicitly off the beaten path. They loved each other and fell asleep clinging together in each other's arms.

The food tasted better. The birds sang more beautifully. The views were breathtaking. Everything became more alive when Raven got to experience it with Kit, and the day they arrived at the foot of Mount Katahdin was no different.

They arrived early that morning and Kit laced her hand into Raven's as she asked, "Are you ready for this?"

"Absolutely," she answered. "But first we have to check in at the visitor's center. I'm not doing all of this and *not* being counted in the official thru-hiker registry."

Kit nodded and they found their way to the little building in Baxter State Park where Raven would officially mark the end of her journey. She signed the registry with her hiker number as well as her trail name, and Kit wrote down her trail name as well even though she didn't have an official thru-hiker number.

"Maybe next year we can come back," she said. "I'll pick up the hundred and fifty miles at the beginning I skipped, and you can show me everything I missed after Wind Gap."

"Or maybe next year we can do the Pacific Crest Trail and have a whole new adventure," Raven said. She looked through the registry for a minute or two, then showed it to Kit, saying, "Check it out – Dodger, Break Time and Eagle Scout finished last week."

"Yellow blazing cheaters," Kit said with a laugh. Then she relented and said, "I'm glad they finished."

Then the two of them went back to the base of Mount Katahdin. The trail was a seventeen-mile loop that would take them to the top of the mountain and back down to their starting point, and compared to everything else Raven had done in the last six months, it seemed almost anti-climactic. There were day hikers setting out on the trip as well, just like there had been when she and Kit climbed Clingman's Dome, and none of them seemed to be feeling the weight of the trail the way that Raven was.

She was glad to have Kit by her side. They took out

their trekking poles and began the hike that would take them through the very last steps of their journey.

Kit talked about Dodger and his Merry Men for the first mile or so, and Raven told her about the last time she'd seen them in New Jersey.

"Do you think they're going to have a hard time adjusting to life beyond the AT?" Kit asked, and Raven shook her head.

"They seem pretty malleable," Raven said. "I'm sure they'll be just fine wherever they land."

"And so will we," Kit said. Raven nodded and knew that it was true.

Much of the Katahdin trail was rocky and sunny, with areas of steep inclines and other stretches where the ground was flat and they passed through the woods. They approached the summit in the early afternoon, and Kit ran up to Raven, grabbing her arm and bouncing excitedly as she pointed and said, "Look! I can see the sign!"

The northern terminus of the Appalachian Trail was marked with a big wooden sign mounted on an A-frame that nestled into the rocks at the very top of the mountain. Raven could just see it from where they were part of the way up the final hill, and as soon as Kit pointed it out, a huge wave of relief washed over Raven.

"We did it," she said. "Come on, I have to touch that sign."

Kit laughed, and they hurried up the final stretch of the hill despite their burning thighs. When they got there, Raven threw her arms around the sign and hugged it, and

Kit borrowed her phone to take a picture of Raven's victory. Then they stood together and took a selfie with the sign in the background and a great expanse of sky behind it all.

"Katahdin at Baxter Peak," Raven read, tracing her fingers over the engraved wooden sign. "Northern terminus of the Appalachian Trail."

"How does it feel?" Kit asked, wrapping her arms around Raven's waist.

"Incredible," Raven said, putting her arm around Kit's shoulder. She looked out at the mountains around her, a 360-degree view that was like looking out at the whole world all at once. "Holy crap, it feels incredible."

She kissed Kit passionately, celebrating every moment of their journey together. Kit laughed and kissed her back, and after a few minutes, another hiker approached the hill and they separated.

"Are you a thru-hiker?" Kit asked him as he came to the sign.

"Yeah," he said. "What about you two?"

"She is," Kit said. "I'm just along for the ride."

"You are, too," Raven said. "Just because you didn't hike every mile, your journey still counts."

"Well, congratulations," the guy said. Kit high-fived him, and then Raven did the same. He looked out over the mountain and pumped his fist in the air, then screamed, "I did it!"

His voice carried on the wind and Raven felt herself getting pumped about her accomplishment all over again, feeding off of his excitement. She and Kit both shouted into the wind, too, and then he looked at them both sort of sheepishly.

"I've been planning to do that ever since Georgia," he said.

"You got a camera?" Kit asked. "Do it again and I'll video it for you."

He handed her his phone and she recorded him shouting his victory at the mountain, then passed the phone back and the three of them sat down on an outcropping of rocks to drink some water and enjoy the moment. After about ten minutes, he got up and said he was going back down the other side of the Katahdin loop.

"You better not stay up here too long," he warned. "It'll be dark before you know it."

"We'll get back on the trail soon," Raven promised, but she put her arm around Kit's shoulder and stayed where she sat on the rock. Their new friend made his way down the slope on the other side of the summit, and when they were alone again, Raven told Kit, "Thank you for being here with me. If I made it all the way here and I was still Lone Wolf, this moment would be meaningless. It means a lot that you're here."

"I'll go anywhere with you," Kit said. "I love you."

Raven took Kit's face in her hands and kissed her again. Then she looked into her big blue eyes and said, "I love you, too."

They sat on the rock for about ten more minutes, rehydrating and eating granola bars to give them energy for the easier hike back down the mountain. Then Raven stood and took Kit's hand, pulling her to her feet.

"Shall we go?"

"I'm ready," Kit said.

As they headed back down the mountain, Raven felt like the pack she'd been carrying on her back for the last six months was weightless. She felt like gravity had lost all meaning and she could see endlessly into the future, with Kit standing right by her side. She twined her fingers into Kit's and they walked side-by-side back down the mountain, back to the new sense of life and home that they'd created together.

Raven called her parents when they were about an hour away from the start of the trail loop, and they were waiting when Kit and Raven returned. She felt tears welling in the back of her throat the moment she saw them, and Kit tried to step back and let them reunite without getting in the way but Raven wouldn't let go of her hand. So they walked together to meet Raven's parents, and her mom circled both of them in her arms.

"I missed you so much, honey," she said, pressing her cheek to Raven's and hugging her tighter than she'd done in the last three years. No more tentative embraces, designed to comfort without hurting her. Raven choked back a tear, but it fell the moment her mom turned to Kit and said, "I've heard so much about you and I'm so glad we can finally meet the girl who stole our daughter's heart."

"Mended it," Raven corrected. "Kit didn't steal anything."

"Thanks for all the candy and food along the trail," Kit said as soon as Raven's mom finally let them both out of her embrace. "I'd love to treat you all to dinner as a proper thank you tonight."

"I like her," Raven's dad said, and they laughed, then he pulled Raven into a hug and said, "It's good to have you back, sweetie. Did you get what you were looking for out there?"

Raven glanced at Kit, then said, "Absolutely."

EPILOGUE

It was the beginning of summer again, and Kit could hardly believe an entire year had gone by since she and Raven met on the Appalachian Trail.

She was standing in the camping section of the enormous outdoor shop where she worked in Chicago, helping a family of four decide on the right sleeping bag for their preteen son. He was about to go on his first camping trip with friends and Kit had been inundating them with the camping knowledge that she'd gotten rather proficient with over the last year.

"This bag is mummy style, which means you can zip it all away up around your neck and it'll keep the cold out at night. The downside is that it can get pretty toasty in there, and it might be a bit much if you're planning to use it in the dog days of summer," she was saying. Then she noticed how bewildered the kid's poor mother looked and Kit scaled it back. She pointed to a standard, inexpensive option. "For the money and in this climate, I'd probably go with this one for your first sleeping bag. You'll probably need to replace it with something sturdier and more weather-resistant if you end up really liking the camping experience, but it's a good starter bag."

"What do you think?" the kid's dad asked, and Kit watched with a smile as the boy ran his hand along the soft surface of the bag, examining all the different colors available.

"I like the blue one," he said after a minute, and his dad pulled it off the shelf and handed it to him.

"Thank you," the kid's mom said. "You've been so helpful – I'm sure we'll be back to talk to you if we think of anything else he needs."

"A good canteen is always a sound investment," Kit said. "And don't forget the sleeping pad – the ground is a lot harder than it looks."

The family wandered up the aisle toward a row of canteens hanging from hooks, and Kit watched them for a moment with satisfaction. The kid was hugging his new sleeping bag to his chest and he had a huge grin on his face.

Kit had been working at the sporting goods store for about six months, and she found that she really had a knack for helping people. She worked her way up to the camping department head in just a few months thanks to the experience she'd gotten on the trail with Raven, and helping people find the right equipment to enjoy the great outdoors turned out to be more rewarding than any data entry or filing temp job she'd ever had.

It wasn't the type of work Kit expected for herself if

she'd had to guess her profession ten years ago, or even five, but it was rewarding and she was good at it. She and Raven had spent nearly every long weekend and holiday over the past year hiking and camping their way through all the parks in the area, and now Kit could name every brand and variation of camping equipment the store sold, their pros and cons, and provide recommendations from personal experience.

She loved it, and she loved the life she was building here with Raven.

She'd come home with Raven and her family after they finished the Appalachian Trail and spent two weeks finding an apartment to share with Raven. They moved all of Raven's things out of storage, and then when the fall semester began and Raven had to go back to work, Kit flew home and packed up her things to move to Chicago permanently.

It had been sad to say goodbye to her parents. She'd lived with them for most of her life, but there was a new adventure calling her, and she promised that she'd come home to see them a few times a year.

Kit called home regularly and she was proud when she told her parents about the sporting goods job. It was full-time with benefits, a better job than she'd had since she lost Monica, and Kit hadn't even thought about leaving it since she started. She was happier now, with Raven, than she'd ever been, and she knew that she was finally home.

When her shift ended, Kit took the train back to her apartment.

Raven wasn't home yet, which was a little unusual. Her spring semester classes had ended the previous week, and that meant a light week of grading before the summer session began.

Kit went into the kitchen to make herself a snack, then sat down at the dining table to eat. The apartment was somewhat sparsely furnished, primarily because the two of them spent very little time in it. Kit loved the city and she was always dragging Raven to new places and events, or else to the parks where they could get back to their roots together.

When they were in the apartment, they were usually in the bedroom, taking advantage of the huge, soft bed that they'd bought together, their first major purchase as a couple living in the real world.

Kit was just finishing the bowl of instant rice she'd made when she heard Raven's key in the lock and her heart leaped into her throat like it always did when saw Raven after even a short absence. She got up and met Raven at the door, putting her arms around her shoulders and kissing her.

"Welcome home," she said. "I missed you."

"I missed you, too, baby," Raven said. She grinned big and said, "I have a surprise for you."

"Oh yeah?" Kit asked.

"You've got three weeks of vacation banked, right?" Raven asked.

"I do," Kit answered, beginning to smile. She liked the direction this was headed.

"I want you to take them all," Raven said. "We're going on an adventure."

"What about your summer classes?" Kit asked.

"I decided not to teach any," Raven said. "It's been too long since we did something big and I'm itching to take you on the road."

"Well, I like the sound of that," Kit said. She stepped closer to Raven, their hips connecting as Raven put her arms around her. "Where are we going?"

"I thought we'd go to North Carolina first," Raven said. "We haven't visited your parents since Christmas and I'm sure they'd love to see you. Then after that? Anywhere you want. And we're going to do it in style."

She pulled a keychain out of her pocket and held it up for Kit to see.

"What did you do?" Kit asked, her eyes going wide.

"I'll show you," Raven said. "Come outside."

RAVEN LED Kit by the hand to the parking lot behind their apartment building. She was grinning from ear to ear as she put her hands over Kit's eyes in the lobby, then she led Kit carefully outside.

"Are you ready?" she asked.

"I'm a little nervous," Kit said. "Who is this spontaneous Raven?"

"She's fun, right?" Raven asked with a delighted laugh. Kit agreed, then Raven uncovered her eyes. "Tada!"

In front of them, there was a boxy, tan recreational vehicle that Raven had been lucky to fit into the small parking lot where space was at a premium. Kit's eyes went even wider and she asked, "You bought an RV?"

Raven laughed and said, "Not exactly. I borrowed it from a friend of my dad's. He said we could have it for the weekend, and I made plans with him to borrow it for a longer trip later in the summer when you get your vacation scheduled. What do you think?"

"I think you're crazy," Kit said, but she was smiling. "You can drive that thing?"

"Not very well," Raven admitted. "But it's basically just a big pickup truck. We'll get used to it as we go. I thought we could take it out to Chain O' Lakes State Park this weekend for a little RV camping getaway, and then we'll plan something bigger for our next trip. Do you like the idea?"

"I love it," Kit said, and Raven smiled.

"Good," she said. "I've been working on getting us the RV for a couple of weeks."

"So, can I get the tour?" Kit asked.

"Of course," Raven said. She led Kit over to the RV, which was taking up two parking spaces and hanging out slightly into the lane behind it. She'd had a little trouble parking the monster, but she was confident that she'd get the hang of it with a little practice. She unlocked the door and held it open for Kit to step up, then followed her and closed the door behind them.

The RV was an older model, small, with a small kitchenette area and a dining table that turned into the bed. It was a little bit cramped, but it was all Raven and Kit needed, especially after spending six months carrying their lives on their backs, and it would take them wherever they wanted to go together.

Kit walked up the aisle, taking everything in, while Raven watched nervously and waited for her reaction. When she finally turned back around, Raven had to ask. "Well?"

Kit grinned, then asked, "Where's the bed?"

Raven raised an eyebrow, then said, "Help me lift the tabletop."

They pulled it off the aluminum table legs that supported it, then Raven moved the legs aside. At her instruction, they set the tabletop back down between the bench seats, and she got a thick cushion from its storage spot in a small closet, laying it down on top of the table's surface to make the bed.

"Very clever," Kit said, but Raven wasn't quite finished.

She grabbed a set of freshly laundered sheets from the closet as well and laid them on the cushions with a flourish, then she asked, "Well, do you want to take our home away from home for a spin?"

"I thought you'd never ask," Kit said as she reached forward and pulled down the curtains on the window above the bed. Raven grabbed Kit in her arms and they flopped down on the bed together.

Kit slid her leg between Raven's thighs, kissing her urgently and running her hands down Raven's body. She arched her back and pressed herself against Kit, seeking her touch. She'd been thinking of little else ever since she took the train across town to pick up the RV, and she had to admit that might have been part of the reason why she had such trouble parking it.

She'd been far too distracted by the possibilities to concern herself with practical matters like that.

Raven pulled Kit's green polo shirt, part of her work uniform, over her head and threw it down on the floor, eager to feel the incredible sensation of their bodies against each other. Kit sat up and took off her sports bra, then worked her fingers quickly down the front of Raven's shirt, popping open the buttons of her blouse.

She spread it open and kissed Raven's breastbone, then the soft, supple flesh of her breast where it was spilling out of the top of her bra. Raven arched her back and Kit slid her hand behind her, unclasping it and pushing it up to reveal her breasts. She'd found a padded variety that gave her a sense of symmetry beneath her clothes and made her feel more confident when she was standing in front of her class or walking around in the world. But when it was just the two of them, Raven felt just as beautiful in nothing as she did in her padded bra.

Maybe more beautiful – she'd never tire of the way that Kit looked at her like she couldn't *wait* to have her.

Raven shimmied out of her shirt and bra and added them to the growing pile of clothes on the floor, then she flipped Kit onto her back and Kit let out a delighted yelp at the sudden movement. Raven knelt on the floor in front of the bed, dragging Kit's knees over the edge of the cushions and then reaching for the button of Kit's khaki pants.

She slid them slowly down over her hips, kissing her stomach and her thighs as she revealed more and more of Kit's body. Then she peeled away her underwear and threw Kit's legs over her shoulders, settling between her thighs.

Raven kissed and licked her, moving her tongue slowly and teasing her until Kit tangled her fingers into Raven's hair and held her mouth against her. Then, when she could taste Kit's need, she started licking and sucking harder, faster.

Kit moved her hips to the rhythm of Raven's tongue, and when Raven slipped one hand through her wetness, she turned her head and gasped against the sheet thrown loosely across the bed. She balled it in her fist and told Raven exactly what she wanted. Raven obliged – touching, kissing, licking, tasting Kit and bringing her to the brink of orgasm. She forgot herself, and everything beyond the bounds of the bed. She closed her eyes and it wasn't hard to imagine that nothing existed except for Kit.

Raven moved her fingers within her, and she circled her tongue tightly against her, bringing Kit into a beautiful release. She moaned loudly and gasped Raven's name, the sound echoing beautifully through the tiny space and bouncing off all the metal surfaces in the little RV.

She couldn't wait to do it all over again in the wilderness, just her, Kit, and a little bit of trail magic.

A NOTE FROM CARA

Hello!

Thanks for reading *Trail Magic* – I hope you enjoyed it!

If you're interested in the research that went into this novel, you can check out my Appalachian Trail Pinterest board at https://www.pinterest.com/lisbonpress/cara-malone-trail-magic/

If you'd like to be notified when I publish a new book, sign up to my newsletter at https://bit.ly/2LPRHXI or connect with me on social media using the icons below.

With love,
Cara

facebook.com/caramalonebooks
twitter.com/caramalonebooks
goodreads.com/caramalonebooks
bookbub.com/authors/cara-malone

LESFIC BOOK CLUB

Calling all lesfic lovers!

Join us for a monthly book club, talk to your favorite lesfic authors, check out our growing community of published and aspiring writers, and hang out in daily chats with fellow lesfic lovers. Check out the group at http://tinyurl.com/lesficlove

ALSO BY CARA MALONE

Avery has spent years getting by all on her own in a big house on the countryside. After watching her elderly neighbor, Nora, be torn away from her long-time lover by heartless relatives, Avery has seen what it's like to love and to lose and she'd rather skip the whole thing... until Nora passes and her great niece Hannah shows up to take care of the house.

This standalone novel - at turns light-hearted and heartbreaking - tells a love story that's two generations in the making.

Read Fixer Upper

SNEAK PEEK: FIXER UPPER

Avery Blake realized too late that her pickup truck wasn't the best-equipped vehicle to transport fragile, old Nora Grayson. First of all, the cab was about two feet higher than Nora could even lift her leg at the age of eighty-four. Avery had to take her by the arm to steady her and then more or less heft her into the seat, noting the papery quality of Nora's skin and worrying that she would hurt her with this motion.

Secondly, there was no good way to secure Nora's oxygen tank and keep it from rolling across the bench seat, so Avery had to keep one hand on the steering wheel and one on the portable oxygen. This task was made all the harder by the fact that Avery hadn't thought to clear out the tools that were always banging around in the foot wells – she really should have planned this outing better, but who plans for a funeral?

She was just thinking that she should have forked over the cash to have Nora transported in some kind of medical van when they pulled into the driveway of Nora's old house. The trip from the nursing home back to Nora's place – right across the street from Avery's house – had been mercifully short, but the journey to the funeral home would be a longer one and Avery wasn't looking forward to juggling the oxygen tank and her octogenarian neighbor – along with her meds and the packrat purse she'd brought along with her – thirty more miles down the road.

"We're home," she said to Nora as she parked the truck and jumped out. Avery walked around to help Nora down, glancing at the house as she went.

It was an old Victorian house with peeling yellow clapboard and lots of ornate details that had been succumbing to dry rot in the years that the house stood empty. Avery spent a lot of time on her porch in the summers, and therefore a lot of time watching the gradual decay of the house across the street. She wasn't sure she wanted to bring Nora back here and let her see what had become of it, but Nora insisted. She wanted to find something of Minnie's to remember her by, and Avery knew Nora's good-for-nothing kids couldn't be bothered to bring her here. They weren't even going to the funeral.

Avery helped Nora down, leaving the oxygen tank momentarily behind and letting Nora lean heavily on her arm as they made the short walk from the truck to the house.

"It's not very pretty anymore, is it?" Nora asked, sounding a little winded as they reached the top of the three creaky steps onto the porch. "Just like me, old and decrepit."

"Stop," Avery scolded, patting Nora on the back of her hand. "It just needs a little love."

The foyer was dark and Avery could see the dust stirring in the air as their steps disturbed it from the floor. It was hard to believe that Nora had only been gone two years – the house felt ancient and forgotten, and the sheets that had been draped over the furniture had a thick layer of dust on them.

"Do you know what you're looking for?" Avery asked.

There were a lot of dusty sheets in the living room alone – Nora lived here almost fifty years, first with her husband and then with Minnie, and that was a lot of years to fill a house with the kinds of knickknacks and tchotchkes that she figured Nora would be looking for now. The funeral was in two hours, and Avery was starting to wonder if they had enough time for this detour after all.

"I think there's something in our bedroom," Nora said, and her voice was so frail that Avery had no idea how she could possibly make it up the stairs, let alone endure the next few hours. Minnie had been everything to her and they spent the last fifteen years inseparable until Nora's kids split them up. Nora made a move for the stairs and Avery took her elbow.

"If you tell me what it is I can go up and get it," she offered.

"Thank you, dear," Nora said, "but I'm afraid I'll only know it when I see it."

"Let me help you up the stairs, then," Avery said, walking beside her as they took them one riser at a time.

With Nora's limited strength, it felt like climbing Mount Everest and Avery thought it might be easier to carry her on the way back down. She couldn't weigh more than ninety pounds dripping wet. When they finally reached the landing, Nora gestured for Avery to wait in the hall.

"Do you want me to hold your bag?" Avery asked, reaching for the large purse slung over Nora's shoulder that she hadn't stopped clutching since Avery picked her up from the nursing home.

"No," Nora said. "It's not a burden."

"Okay," Avery said, watching Nora shuffle over to a closed door near the end of the hall. "Holler if you need me."

Nora disappeared into her bedroom, the door swinging almost shut behind her, and Avery stood around in the hall. There was an antique oak credenza opposite the bannister, covered in a thick layer of dust just like everything else, and a mirror that was starting to lose its silver hung above it.

To kill the time, Avery walked over to it and blew a cloud of dust off the glass, stepping out of the way while it settled. Then she stepped back in front of the mirror, inspecting her short, nearly black hair, normally untamed and falling across her forehead, to make sure it was still neatly slicked back. She straightened the tie around her neck and brushed away the wrinkles that had worked their way into her jacket and pants on the ride over.

NORA WENT INTO HER BEDROOM, putting her hand on the dresser by the door for support. Walking through the house and seeing everything covered in sheets had been hard enough, but looking at the bed was something different entirely. She walked over to Minnie's side – always on the right – and ran her hand over the blanket, smoothing it out.

Minnie always made the bed as soon as they got out of it in the mornings, and turned it down meticulously each night. It even used to irritate Nora the way she tucked the sheets so tightly under the mattress. Nora preferred to give her feet a little more freedom to roam in the night... but oh, what she wouldn't give to feel the tightness of the sheets around her toes now.

A plume of dust rose into the air as she tidied the bed, reminding her that it had been two full years since she last slept in it, and three since she shared it with Minnie.

Nora turned away from the bed before the tears had a chance to come. She went back to the dresser by the door. It was covered with a sheet like most everything else in the house, and the top of it was lumpy since whoever closed up the house hadn't taken the time to pack away the knickknacks before covering the furniture. Nora carefully lifted the front of the sheet, more dust flying into the air, and revealed a collection of figurines on top of the dresser, exactly the way she remembered them.

They were Florence ceramics and most of them belonged to Minnie. She started collecting the little ceramic women during the war, while she and Nora were raising their families and their husbands were fighting. The figurines had been an occasional splurge to balance the pressures of working and homemaking and child rearing, and they always lit up Minnie's face whenever she showed off her latest acquisition.

A few of them belonged to Nora, though. Minnie had gifted them to her at a time when symbolic gestures were all they could share, and they continued to mean a lot to Nora. She wanted to bring them with her to the nursing home, but she couldn't bear to separate them from the rest of the collection.

Now, she picked up a figurine in a full-length pink dress and a bonnet decorated with gold foil accents – her name was Clarissa, according to collectors – and wrapped it carefully in a kerchief she brought with her. This was the very first figurine Minnie ever gave her, and it always held a special place in Nora's heart. She tucked it into the bottom of her purse, and then she pulled a small leather journal out of her bag, tucking it into the top drawer of the dresser beneath a pile of neatly folded slacks where she hoped it would be safe.

Then Nora opened the bedroom door and announced into the hall, "Okay, dear, I'm ready. I appreciate your patience with an old woman."

THE FUNERAL WAS SMALL, primarily attended by Minnie's children and grandchildren. They all thanked

Nora for coming out to pay her respects to an old friend, and Avery watched her face carefully for a reaction.

She didn't think she could stand it if she lost someone as close as Minnie had been to Nora and no one even acknowledged her grief, but Nora seemed to take it in stride. They'd hidden their relationship for so many years, Avery figured she was just used to playing the role of the best friend. It was more than Avery would have been able to do.

Nora held it together like a real trooper through the entire funeral service, watching solemnly as the casket was wheeled down the aisle toward the altar and dabbing delicately at the corner of her eyes while the priest spoke. Avery was standing by with tissues and the oxygen tank and a supportive hand if need be, but Nora turned out to be a lot stronger than she looked.

She didn't really break down until they lowered poor Minnie into the ground.

The cemetery was wet with last night's rain and Nora clung to Avery's arm as they walked to the grave site. She thought it was just that the terrain was rough going and Nora's modest one-inch heels were sinking into the earth with every step. It wasn't until the priest said his final prayer over the casket that she realized Nora was clinging to her because Avery was the only thing keeping her from collapsing.

A small yelp, something like a wounded animal would make, came from Nora's lips while everyone else crossed themselves and muttered an *amen*, and then

Avery felt Nora's weight pulling on her arm as her legs went to jelly.

She dropped the oxygen tank to the wet grass and held onto Nora, keeping her on her feet and holding her tight for support as she sobbed. Most everyone headed back to their cars after the casket was lowered, a few of them looking at Nora with a mixture of pity and confusion, and Avery felt the urge to lash out at them rising up in her throat.

Who the hell were they to stare at her grief?

Move it along, asshole, she wanted to growl when their eyes lingered on Nora, and Avery held her tighter to keep her from the realization that she'd become a spectacle for them.

When they got back to the truck, Avery practically carrying Nora across the grounds, she carefully looped the oxygen cannula over Nora's ears and brought it to her nose. Avery gave her a few minutes to settle down before starting the journey back to the nursing home, and the way Nora's face was twisted into a physical manifestation of the pain of losing Minnie really ate at Avery.

In a million years, she couldn't be as strong as Nora had been that day, or as tenacious as she'd been in her love for Minnie all her life. If this was the heartache people signed up for when they fell in love, she didn't want any part of it.

Read Fixer Upper

Printed in Great Britain
by Amazon